"Manfred Krutein knows his U-Boats from first hand experience gained during war patrols in U-123 while serving in Admiral Dönitz' Atlantic Submarine Force. This background provides unique authenticity to the U-Boat setting Krutein has chosen for his gripping and all too plausible tale of Nazi terrorism and desperation at the close of World War II. Suspenseful and fast moving in the Clancy style, HITLER'S LAST GASP will hold his readers, be they sailors or landlubbers, to the last paragraph."

William L. Read
Vice-Admiral, U.S. Navy, Ret.

"HITLER'S LAST GASP is a dramatic fiction which portrays the courage and ingenuity of one of the unknown American heroes in the OSS during WWII. Eric Svensen is the OSS agent who recognizes the significance of U-888's potential for mass destruction and adamantly pursues the submarine, using intelligence networks and his own intuition. This exciting book combines the thrill of the chase with an intimate view of Allied spy and intelligence operations which helped defeat Hitler. If you enjoyed RED OCTOBER, you will want to read this book."

Robert Mulcahy
Historian for Edward Air Force Base, California

"Manfred Krutein's time aboard German U-boats shows on every page of this vivid and exciting suspense novel, which roams from fjords of Norway to the North Atlantic to Cuba, Italy and Mexico, packed with action every step and mile of the way."

Theodore Taylor
Author of TO KILL THE LEOPARD and THE CAY

HITLER'S LAST GASP

The Miracle Weapon

Manfred Krutein

To Bo

Manfred Krutein

Printed in the United States of America
        First Printing, 1995
        ISBN: 0-938513-19-2
        Library of Congress Catalog Number 95-75897

    Cover art: copyright © 1995 by Wernher Krutein - Fotovault
    Technical assistance, Irmgard Ryan

AMADOR PUBLISHERS
P. O. Box 12335
Albuquerque, NM 87195 USA

This book is a work of fiction. In some instances based on fact. Where names of real persons, living or dead, are used the situations, incidents, or dialogues are entirely fictional and are not intended to depict actual events.

To the **SERVAS** Organization, which rose from the ashes of World War II, and its members who are working for peace.

To the SILVA ANO generation, which rose from the ashes of World War II, and its children, who are working for peace

1. Hardanger Fjord, Norway - April 1, 1945.

More than a hundred SS men worked diligently in the secret factory at the Hardanger Fjord. An ear-piercing whistle, followed by a loud "*Achtung!*" echoed through the production hall. Everyone froze, eyes on the open door, hands down.

SS Standartenführer Albert Krantz, his head high as if he ruled the world, strutted in and stopped abruptly. Wearing an immaculate tailored black uniform with a red armband and swastika, he surveyed the hall and shouted: "*Heil* Hitler!" His ambition to rise above his current rank of SS Colonel led him to use every opportunity to show his unbending devotion to Hitler.

"*Heil* Hitler!" the men shouted in response.

Production manager Stolz, a stubby, pale-faced man in a black uniform jacket, riding-breeches and lacquered boots, stepped forward and lifted his arm in the Nazi salute. "SS Major Stolz reports 112 SS men assigned to 'Operation *FEUER ALARM.*'"

Glancing at the men, the *Standartenführer* yelled: "Keep working!"

Krantz then looked at Stolz, his eyes as cold as the fjord water. "Everything progressing as planned?"

"*Jawoll, Standartenführer.*"

Stolz pointed to a row of large gray cylinders. "Ten containers ready to be loaded." His finger moved at the side bay. "Spare parts over there."

"Any failures or sabotage?" Krantz asked. Sabotage was rampant in Norway in the spring of 1945. The resistance fought against the German occupiers.

"*Nein, Standartenführer.*"

"Did you test all weapon launchers?"

"*Jawoll, Standartenführer.*"

"What results?"

"Every launcher was tested three times, each time with excellent success."

"So? Who's your test engineer? I want to talk to him."

"SS Commander Gebhardt."

Stolz beckoned to Gebhardt, who rushed forward lifting his arm in a brisk salute. He was a white-haired man; his lab coat was spotted all over, his fingers dirty.

Krantz looked at him with distaste. "How did the tests go? Any mishaps?"

"I changed the faulty erector spindles to make them function properly. Several ignitors failed and were replaced."

"Can you guarantee them?"

"*Nein, Standartenführer.*"

"Why not?"

"Too little time! Assembly time is too short..."

"Are you criticizing your superiors?" Krantz yelled, his fingers spread apart like spider legs.

"There's not enough time for testing the..."

"Oh?" Krantz interrupted. His eyes narrowed. "Not enough time?"

"The operation is insane —"

"You're arrested!" Krantz shouted. Turning to his adjutant, he ordered: "To Neuengamme! There he will learn to obey." Looking at the SS workers who stared at him in shock, he barked to Stolz, "This is a project the *Führer* gave top priority. I expect everyone to work day and night. All launchers must be tested again. Beginning now!"

A few minutes later Krantz left the room. Neuengamme was a cruel concentration camp. Now the workers understood the seriousness of this mission.

2. Wilhelmshaven, Germany - April 1, 1945.

In the muddy water that flowed from the Jade River into the lock chamber, a blue-gray submarine lay tied to the pier, ready to leave. The water between the two gates of the lock gradually rose to the level of the outside sea. Countless U-boats and war ships of the *Kriegsmarine* had passed through these gates to spread fear and terror over the Atlantic Ocean.

Boatswain Hans Hartmann, heavy-built with the round face of an East German, made a last-minute check of the sub's upper deck. He gave instructions to six sailors on the slippery deck. "Stay here to handle the lines. We'll leave any moment." Hartmann then climbed to the conning tower and stood before the First Watch Officer (1WO), Lieutenant Helms, saluting as he reported, "Everything on deck inspected. Boat is ready to depart."

The 1WO wanted to make his report to the skipper, *Kapitänleutnant* Hans Brinker, who had heard everything and said to both, "*Danke*, we must wait. Just received a phone call from Berlin. A new operation order."

Brinker's white cap cover showed that he was the *Kommandant.* The crew saw him as the typical blond, North-German naval officer of average height in his early thirties. He radiated assertiveness, authority and shrewdness, giving his officers and men confidence in his leadership.

He and four others in the bathtub-like bulwark of the conning tower, wore gray leather coats that reached down over their rubber boots. Wide-brimmed sou'westers protected the sailors against the cold drizzle. Towels, jammed in the open space on their necks, prevented rain from seeping down their backs.

Brinker turned to the first watch officer, "Do we have enough ack-ack ammo?"

"*Jawoll, Herr Kaleu.*" Helms used the abbreviation for the skipper's rank, regularly applied by the crew in brief answers. "Stowed under deck, guns loaded."

"We'll have only three minesweepers for air protection," the skipper said. "We'd better man both guns."

"Yes, sir." Lanky Helms had to bend his knees to meet the height restriction for submariners. He yelled down through the hatch, "Gun crews to the tower!"

For the hundredth time Brinker thought to himself, Lieutenant Helms was a reliable officer. Brinker had kept him on board the submarine for ten patrols. They had been together in many convoy battles and depth charge attacks.

To relieve his men from the obvious impatience of waiting to leave port, Brinker called out to one of the two sailors standing at the rear end of the turret. "Lembke, what's the news of your family?"

The sailor stopped blowing on his cold hands. "My wife and the two little ones are in Bremen. They left Königsberg by ship."

"They were lucky to escape the Russians, eh?" the *Kommandant* said. His right hand wiped water droplets from his chin.

"Yessir, I'm grateful." Lembke sighed. "My wife wrote there were nine thousand people aboard the BERLIN, mostly women and children, all fleeing from East Prussia to the West."

Brinker turned to Boatswain Hartmann. "Did *your* family leave Danzig?"

"Yes, sir. They're in Oldenburg. They stood on the deck of a minesweeper for two days and nights. So many people on the ship."

Brinker nodded. "I guess it's the same story everywhere, once the Russians advanced on Danzig. At least our families are safe. We've lost everything else."

"The Red Army advanced so fast," Lembke grumbled. "Where is the *Wunderwaffe?* Hitler said it's ready for the final victory. When will he use it?"

The "Miracle Weapon" was Lembke's favorite topic. The others did not reply. They detested Nazi party propaganda.

Brinker studied the activity on the pier. If the new operation order was so damned urgent, why wasn't someone delivering it?

The sub was ready, the men were ready... He remembered yesterday's talk with Lembke who had joined the crew just a week ago. The sailor was surprised about the camaraderie that he had never experienced on a big cruiser. "I think everyone likes me," Lembke had said.

Brinker had answered, "We're a team. Otherwise we can't stand each other in this cramped boat."

Kapitän Werner, the flotilla commander, and his adjutant stood on the pier beside the submarine. Werner raised his left arm and pushed back the sleeve of his dark-blue coat. He peered at his watch, then called to Brinker. "They should be here any moment."

"I hope so," Brinker yelled back. "Little good news came from the *BdU* (*Befehlshaber der Unterseeboote*, Commander-in-Chief of U-boats) nowadays."

Werner and his adjutant paced up and down the pier, conferring in lowered voices as they walked, angered by the delay.

The *Kommandant* watched the sailors standing on deck, waiting to handle the lines. They looked bored. He thought of Ursula, his wife. What would happen to her when the British army reached Hamburg? What would happen to our families as the war dragged on? Walter Schramm, the navigator, had a home on the western side of the Rhine River. He'd no news of his wife and children since the Americans occupied that sector.

On the pier, the eight armed sailors guarding the submarine snapped to attention as a Volkswagen command car drove up. The vehicle braked to a stop and an SS officer quickly stepped out. Tall and slim like all Hitler's bodyguards, wearing an overlong black coat, a knight's cross just showing at his neck, the man glared at the flotilla commander. Then he clicked the heels of his shining boots, "*Sturmbannführer* Gockel from *Führer* Headquarters. Are you *Kapitän* Werner?"

"Werner," said the flotilla commander.

"I have important documents for *Kapitänleutnant* Brinker."

"He's waiting for you. I'll call him down."

"No! I'll go aboard."

Werner raised a hand to stop him. "Sorry, no one except the crew is allowed on board a boat that's about to leave port."

"I am the representative of the *Führer*!" Gockel shouted. He moved toward the submarine.

The sailor guarding the gangway stepped forward, rifle in both hands. "*Halt*! No access to the U-boat."

The SS officer stopped, outraged.

Brinker called over: "I'll come ashore." He stepped to the gangway. "Brinker," he said, putting himself between the sailor and the SS officer.

"*Sturmbannführer* Gockel from *Führer* Headquarters. I'm not used to being treated this way." Taking a deep breath, he continued. "I have important documents for *Kapitänleutnant* Brinker." He eyed the front of Brinker's salt-crusted leather coat. "I was told the *Kapitänleutnant* wears the knight's cross. You have none. I must see your I.D."

"We never wear such things on board," Brinker answered. "We don't have I.D.s; we know each other. May I have the documents?"

Gockel looked at the U-boat with arrogance before he continued, "I can't waste any more time. Here's a top secret order co-signed by the commander-in-chief of U-boats. You have the honor of being selected for a very important mission. Do not open this envelope until two hours after you leave port. Only *you* are authorized to open it. Is that understood? You will sign this receipt."

Brinker wondered why an SS officer delivered the new operation order. What had the SS to do with a U-boat? And what a pompous ass Gockel was.

The skipper clamped the envelope under his left arm and scribbled his signature on the receipt.

Werner asked Gockel if he had a copy for the flotilla staff.

"*Nein, Herr Kapitän*, there is only an original of this order. Not even the *BdU* has a copy. A new number has been assigned to the boat, U-888. All operation orders are being worked out by the *Führer* Headquarters. You are not priviledged to see them. Heil Hitler!"

He clicked his heels, shot his right arm into the air, turned around and walked stiffly to the car. "Back to the airport!" he ordered the driver.

Engine howling, the vehicle moved away, the tires spraying water over the wet pier.

Werner said, "Arrogant bastard!" Then looked with embarrassment at Brinker. "Sorry. I've a short temper these days. Orders from Berlin are especially aggravating. What is so secret that I'm not allowed to know?"

Brinker pushed his cap up and shook his head. "I have no idea. So far, all we've recently received from Berlin is nonsense. Pure *Quatsch*. And now this! Since when is the SS involved in naval affairs? If the *BdU* hadn't co-signed, I wouldn't open it."

"I no longer understand what's going on in Berlin," said Werner with a sigh. "The top party members are desperate. Anyway, I wish you the best."

With a half salute to his superior, Brinker grinned and said: "Report U-888 ready to sail."

Werner managed a wink. "Good luck and happy return."

A few minutes later the submarine left the lock, carefully threading its way between the buoys that marked the deep-water channel.

Soon U-888 was joined by five minesweepers waiting a mile from the lock. They quickly moved in front of the sub to protect it from contact mines. Fifteen minutes later, an anti-mine warfare ship — a large freighter — approached. Filled with thousands of empty barrels to keep it afloat in case of a hit by a mine, it maneuvered ahead of the little convoy to destroy magnetic and sophisticated electronic mines. Four small fishing trawlers appeared and grouped themselves around the submarine to provide anti-aircraft fire. For camouflage, all vessels had irregular dark and bright spots on their gray-painted hulls. The colors of water, sky, ships and U-boat blended into shades of gray, a ghostly caravan on a mission of destruction in the North

Atlantic.

The clouds lowered to about three hundred feet over the water and a heavy rain shower engulfed the ships. Brinker could barely see the five minesweepers in front of the U-boat. Binoculars were no longer useful. Soaked, the men at the ack-ack guns turned their backs to the wind and rain. Brinker ordered: "Gun crews below deck!"

The eight men squeezed forward to the hatch in the conning tower and disappeared one by one into the boat.

Brinker turned to Helms, the first watch officer: "Didn't Werner tell us we'd have only three minesweepers for protection? Who ordered the other vessels?"

"Who knows? A top man from Berlin comes to the pier, dressed in black like the devil. Only a brass band was missing," the tall first watch officer said. "I'm curious about what's in the envelope."

Strange that so many ships were escorting the boat. What game was Berlin playing this time?

An hour later the trawlers and minesweepers turned away and let the sub pass them. Their crews, standing on deck, waved to the submariners. A short time later the freighter veered away, signaling goodbye with a lamp, *AUF WIEDERSEHEN*. A few minutes later the freighter disappeared in the rain and U-888 continued alone through the rough North Sea.

Kapitänleutnant Brinker gave precise instructions to the second watch officer, who would take over the conning tower. Then he asked Schramm, the navigator, "Any questions about the course?"

"No, sir. All clear."

The skipper turned to Helms, "I want to see you in ten minutes." Then he went to the hatch and yelled, "*Abwärts!* — Downward!" and disappeared into the boat.

Helms followed the skipper without delay. Passing through the officers' wardroom, he saw the *Kommandant* still in his wet clothes holding the envelope and calling for a cup of coffee.

Helms undressed. Taking the towel from around his neck, he

wrung it out and hung it and his wet coat on a clothes hanger on the wall where the water dripped to the floor. Toweling off his face and hands, he pulled on a dry sweater. Then he went to the galley for a cup of hot coffee. He warmed his cold hands on the thick porcelain cup and saw the skipper studying the contents of the manila envelope. The *Kommandant* looked up and handed the paper to Helms. "Read it!"

  OPERATION FEUER ALARM - Order No. 1

Helms scowled. "'Fire alarm.' What does that mean? Who's going to set a fire?"

"Read on," the skipper said, watching the first watch officer's face.

> "...former march order modified. U-888 will march to Hardanger Fjord, Southern Norway. AMW-ship SB-16 will await U-888 at the fjord entrance to guide it into the fjord. Tie up alongside Barge CB-23, which will be anchored in the fjord. Floating crane SK-14 will be tied at barge's left side, easily visible. Two navigation charts are enclosed. Further instructions will be received from *Kapitän zur See* Bauer who is on board SB-16..."

Brinker could no longer contain his anger. "They give us a 'march order' as if we are to march over the North Sea like Jesus over the Sea of Galilee." He shook his head. "Left side instead of port side. But the *BdU* has signed it in the lower left corner. See?" Frowning, he unfolded two charts: Hardanger Fjord and the surrounding sea off southern Norway. He rubbed his bearded chin. "Unbelievable!"

After a moment of hesitation he called *Obersteuermann* Schramm, the navigator, who had just been relieved from his bridge watch. As Schramm sat down at the table, Brinker explained the new order.

"No problem, *Herr Kaleu*. We'll make it. I'll work out the new course." Schramm, a short man with constantly shifting eyes, took the charts and left for the petty officers' mess.

Brinker spoke into the intercom: "*Kommandant* to all crew members! As most of you know, we received a new order from

Berlin before leaving port. Our boat has a new number, U-888. Instead of operating in the Faeroe Islands region, we're ordered to the Hardanger Fjord in southern Norway. Imagine for a few days that you are on a Norwegian cruise ship. Enjoy. Carry on."

Cheers sounded through the boat. Going to a Norwegian fjord would be a nice change.

3. Bath, England - April 2, 1945.

Equipped with a parachute, the tall OSS Major Erik Svensen stepped aboard a British plane near Bath to be flown over the North Sea. He could easily be recognized as a typical American of Norwegian ancestry. A good-looking man, totally involved in the Great Game of Intelligence, used to a constant inflow of action reports, he felt the uneventful night flight endless. At dusk he was told to prepare for the jump. They had reached the dark Norwegian coast. An air force sergeant checked his parachute again and hooked the rip cord to a bolt near the door. He nodded to Erik, giving him the thumb-up sign and smiled. "Be careful, we're very low!" With caution he opened the door. On the buzzer sign from the pilot, Erik jumped and fell toward the treeless Norwegian rock landscape. A heavy air blast threw him back, producing a short ear-piercing whistle in his ears. The engine and propeller noise stopped. Peng! The parachute opened and jerked him up. His body swung back and forth in the silent, dark air of the night. He remembered to pull up his knees, ready to land. Only moments later he struck the ground with a heavy impact, the chute pulling him to the side. He tried to stand but was pushed twice to the ground. Only then could he free himself from the shrouds. He pulled the dark-green chute together and bundled it into a small package. He took a compass from the small side pocket of his jacket to orient himself. According to the flight plan he should be five miles north of the Hardanger Fjord. There he would find Olaf, the young Norwegian agent, who had sent the urgent radio call yesterday.

In order to reach the fjord and Olaf's hiding place he must hike south. Erik had studied the map so thoroughly that he remembered every detail. He took the radio from the side pocket of his pants. Dammit! It was broken. Ripping off the broken top plate, he saw that the electronic parts and the battery were smashed also. His right thigh still throbbed from his impact with the ground which must have ruined the radio. He hid the silk

bundle under a shrub and buried the radio under pebbles. Should
he now be surprised by German soldiers, he could identify
himself as a uniformed American airman who had parachuted
from a crippled plane. He couldn't be shot as a spy.

Fortunately nobody came along to test this story. An hour
later, after moving as swiftly as he could in the dark, he stood
above the fjord. At the beginning of dawn, he recognized the
curved shore line and figured he must be about two miles to the
west of Olaf's position. He cautiously walked eastward, whistling
from time to time a bird call known to Olaf as a code signal.
When he heard it repeated and louder, he knew he was close to
the young agent. In the man-high shrubs they approached each
other. Erik almost didn't recognize Olaf who was wearing a full
brown beard that covered most of his ruddy, round face.

"Olaf! How are you?" Erik called in Norwegian.

"Did you get my message?" Olaf asked.

"Yes. But what is happening? You didn't make it clear."

Olaf edged back to where they had a complete view of the
fjord and pointed to the factory." See the barge and the floating
crane? They arrived yesterday. With the two tug boats."

"Uu-huh. Looks like they're getting ready to load something."

"Maybe now we'll find out what they're doing over there."

Erik grunted. "If we're lucky. They've managed to keep the
damn place so secret we don't have a clue about what's going on
in that factory. What are they making?"

Olaf shrugged. "It could be almost anything."

Erik asked about the Germans' activities at the factory.

"Three to four trucks arrive every day. They unload inside the
building and leave empty after an hour."

"What else?"

"There are six ambulances. Do you see them to the left of the
factory?"

"Strange," Erik said. "Why do they need that many? Did they
ever use them?"

"Three weeks ago. An accident. Four of them drove away.
Thirty men rushed out of the building. With gas masks over their

heads. Stood in the yard for three hours."

"With the gas masks on?"

"Yes. All men in white coats."

"I don't like the sound of that. Got good binoculars?"

"The best, Zeiss." Olaf handed Erik the gray Zeiss, which Erik used immediately to look at the factory.

"These are damned good! Loot from the Germans?"

Olaf nodded. "My brother stole them from the Krauts. Hey! Look at the truck driving from the factory to the pier. See?"

For two hours Erik watched the Germans carefully load long metal containers, ten in number, from the factory to the barge. The containers were about twenty-five feet long with a diameter of three feet.

"Any idea what they could be?" Erik asked.

Olaf slowly shook his head.

"We'd better call the bombers."

"Did you bring new batteries for my radio?" Olaf asked.

"Batteries? Your message didn't say anything about batteries."

The young Norwegian looked embarrassed. "I couldn't remember the code letter for batteries. I called for 'juice' in my report."

"Crap! I didn't understand that. My radio was smashed when I landed. The battery too, and I didn't bring extras. Are yours down?"

"Hell! What do we do now?" Olaf lamented.

A soft humming noise came up from the fjord. Olaf and Erik looked below and saw three freighters painted gray with irregular dark spots for camouflage, sailing into the fjord, ack-ack guns prominently displayed.

"All manned. Ready to shoot," Olaf said.

Erik figured the size of the steamers at 5,000 to 8,000 tons. Did the Germans need these ships to carry away the containers on the barge? Why so many ships? His mind raced with possibilities as he watched the vessels anchor near the factory.

Damn it to hell! Now was the time to call in the bombers to destroy everything the Nazis had brewed up down there. And they had no working radio.

"Listen, Olaf! The only way to reach our bombers is to call from Bergen. I want you to walk to the resistence center in Bergen and report what's going on," Erik said. "We must get the bombers up here." Seeing Olaf's long face he asked, "What's wrong?"

"It's eight to ten hours to Bergen. That's a long walk."

"Then you better get started. These ships down there aren't going to wait for us."

Sullenly Olaf agreed. "By the way, Per will be here in two days to bring new food. He has a radio on his boat."

"On the BIRGIT?"

Olaf nodded, pointing to a small tool shack sitting back on the edge of the fjord wall. "There's still food and water for a few days. And two blankets. You can also change clothes and wear my fisherman's outfit if you like."

"*Adiø*!" Erik said as Olaf disappeared behind the shrubs. Erik sat down on the slope, roughly 300 feet above the fjord. More waiting! This damn war. It was all hurry up and wait. He thought of the OSS office in England, where agents like himself worked to analyze intelligence reports and to plan new espionage activities on the continent. They were waiting for his message to send bombers to destroy the mysterious factory in the Hardanger fjord.

4. Hardanger Fjord, Norway - April 3, 1945.

Five officers jumped up from their chairs as SS *Standartenführers* Albert Krantz and Georg Schmeltzer entered the manager's office in the fjord factory. Krantz, the senior, surveyed the officers with a questioning look.

Krantz stepped to the wall for a look at the map of the fjord. "The loading site is well selected. Bombers won't have a chance." He turned to one of the five officers. "Are all containers on the barge?"

"Yes, *Standartenführer*."

Krantz wiped a speck of dust from his black uniform, carefully avoiding the gold-rimmed party badge which showed he was one of Hitler's party comrades of the 'Old Guard,' those men who started the Nazi party in the 1920s. He was tense. Was everything done to make Operation *FEUER ALARM* a success? he thought. He hadn't selected the five men who formed his team. Could he trust Schmeltzer who had trained them to deploy the weapon?

Suddenly his hand slammed on the fjord map, killing a fly that had just landed. He smiled grimly as the tiny body fell to the floor. He stepped on it and twisted his foot. Typical Albert Krantz. Wiping his hand on a clean white handkerchief, he turned back to his officers. "Go over the instructions one more time in the next two hours!"

Standartenführer Schmeltzer stepped forward, his jacket pressed tightly around his moon-shaped belly. He rubbed his thick hands for a while, then looked for a moment into his open right hand as if to see into the future. For the next ten minutes he briefed the team again. Finally, looking up into their eyes he said: "Now is the moment for me to say 'Good-by' to you. Our nation expects the final victory from you. I've carefully planned the operation and I trust you. Devote your life to our revered *Führer* and the fatherland." Arm raised perpendicular to his body, his heels clicked. "*Heil* Hitler!"

15

5. Hardanger Fjord, Norway - April 3, 1945.

Erik Svensen sat at the bend of the fjord, binoculars trained on the ships below him. Still anchored in the bay, the barge floated just in front of him, the ten gray cylinders still neatly stacked on its deck. And the Allied bombers had not shown up as yet.

He rubbed his eyes, having slept little since his arrival. But he had taken the time to bury his uniform and was now wearing Olaf's fisherman clothes and a camouflage overall. Happy to have escaped the staff work in Bath where the American OSS group worked with MI-5 on activities on the continent, he was in Norway, the country of his ancestors. And he was near the enemy he had to observe. For a long time he had wished to be in this situation. At this moment he alone was responsible for the destruction of the secret factory and the product of several months that was loaded on the barge. Too bad he had to wait for the BIRGIT to use the radio!

At noon another freighter steamed into the fjord, then a German U-boat. Adrenaline pumped through his veins, he suddenly forgot how tired he was. Through the binoculars he watched the submarine move alongside the barge and tie up. Dammit! Where were those bombers?

A motorboat left the side of the freighter and made the short run to the submarine. Erik followed the boat's movements and saw a naval officer board the sub. The officer disappeared down the ladder into the bowels of the U-boat. Erik turned his binoculars to the submarine crew working on deck. The sailors busied themselves removing several deck plates along both sides. The floating crane swung toward the sub, its long arm slowly deliberate as it raised ten cigar-shaped containers, one at a time, from the sub's open deck spaces and put each on one side of the barge. Then the crane picked up the first of the cylinders delivered from the factory, swung back to the submarine and placed it in one of the emptied spaces below deck of the superstructure.

Erik was surprised to see the shipment loaded onto a submarine. For what reason? Why a sub? Notebook in lap, he hurriedly scribbled notes describing what he had seen. Each detail might be important.

Two hours later, when the loading of the cylindrical containers was finished, the sub's sailors put the deck plates back in place and bolted them tight. Ten cylinders had been stowed below deck, five on each side in a line from bow to stern.

The motorboat that had been alongside the sub made a quick trip to the factory and returned with ten men in black uniforms.

Erik swore under his breath. SS men? Hitler's political troop? For ten minutes the men stood on the bow of the sub, conversing with the naval officer from the freighter and a short man in a gray jacket and a white cap. Erik wished to hear their conversation.

The sun broke through the clouds and the whole area below was bathed in light. With Olaf's powerful Zeiss binoculars, he was able to make out even more details. Four of the black-clad men carried kitbags and crates from the motorboat to the deck of the U-boat. He counted four wooden crates, about two by two by six feet each, and six kitbags. Sailors lifted the gear through a hatch close to the bow into the sub. When everything had been loaded, the naval officer from the freighter and four of the black-clad men raised their arms in a Nazi salute, climbed into the motorboat and left for the factory. Six SS men stayed on the sub.

Sailors on the barge pulled the gangplank from the submarine and threw off the lines. The U-boat, free, moved slowly away from the barge. The personnel on the barge and the sub exchanged farewell waves. In contrast, the six black-uniformed men on the sub lifted their arms in a stiff salute. Certainly SS! Erik thought.

Forming a convoy around the submarine, the four freighters moved down the fjord to the ocean. All anti-aircraft guns manned and ready.

He looked at his wristwatch. 4:15 p.m. Why hadn't the Allied bombers appeared? Olaf should have reached Bergen hours ago.

Why wasn't the damned submarine and its convoy being blown out of the water right now? He sighed. Something could have happened to Olaf. Or maybe the bombers were too busy for a run over southern Norway? There were any number of possible explanations. He wished he was on Per's boat so he could follow the convoy and make a brief radio report. Surely his colleagues from the OSS and MI-5 of the British Intelligence Service in Bath would be eager to hear about the U-boat. Every minute without his transmitter made his being here absolutely useless. He might as well be blind, deaf and dumb.

Carefully, he climbed down toward the spit where he would meet Per's boat. One false step and the gravel would slide out from under his shoes. He lost his balance and fell against a boulder, scraping his elbow and knee. Trying to keep himself from falling farther, he grabbed at a shrub — slipping — slipping — there! His fall checked, he looked down. Had the Germans on the barge seen him? He could see no commotion on the barge. When his breathing returned to normal, he again began as quietly as he could to reach the rocks at the water level.

Arriving at the spit he squatted down to wait for the boat. Why did the Krauts load the cylinders on a U-boat? We were sinking so many subs in the Atlantic. Maybe they would transport them to a German port. But why?

Then he heard the distinctive diesel sound of a small boat. To his surprise it stayed away from the shore line and passed the spit without stopping.

He stood up and waved frantically. The boat continued into the fjord, its motor chugging rhythmically.

Erik sank down behind a rock. Of course! It was too bright for Per to stop at the spit in full sight of the German barge. Damn it! More valuable time lost! He felt the cold of the ground creep into his body. The sun had set and twilight shrouded the majestic fjord. He opened his knapsack, took out the last chocolate bar, peeled off the paper and chewed the chocolate slowly.

He considered his position. If necessary, he could bed down on the spit, although it would be even colder than his tool shed higher up. And if Per didn't come back, he could hike to Bergen, just as Olaf had done. But then his information about the submarine and its mysterious cargo would be delayed even longer.

Seething with impatience, he paced along the spit, stumbling over rocks in the dark, but too agitated to sit still. Suddenly he heard the noise of a stuttering diesel. He stopped. It was Per's boat. This time it stopped. Erik's watch showed 6:59 p.m. He called quietly to Per standing at the bow: "Erik Svensen here! Olaf went to Bergen. Pick *me* up!"

Per, surprised, waved. He knew Erik from previous intelligence activities. A moment later Erik was on board the BIRGIT.

6. Off Norway - April 3, 1945.

Leaving Hardanger Fjord, the convoy and U-888 took a course north toward Trondheim, staying together for three hours. Then the four armed freighters turned around and their crews waved good-by to the submariners.

The U-boat was alone again, just as it had been during the five years of the war.

Kapitänleutnant Brinker, one of the few remaining U-boat aces who had been decorated by the *Führer* with the Oak Leaves to the Knights' Cross, knew he should dive as soon as possible to check the sub's buoyancy after taking on ten new containers and six crates. They had simply exchanged the useless torpedo containers with similar ones with a lifting rack on one end. In 1945 it was too dangerous to transfer torpedoes from deck to boat in the North Atlantic. The *Kommandant* felt it was imperative to have the boat in top diving condition. Always alert, he cared for his boat and crew, the mark of a successful skipper. He looked with pride from the conning tower down on his boat that was sailing with smooth rolling motions through the water.

"Alarm! Diving!" he yelled. Automatically, the bridge crew jumped one at a time down through the small turret hatch into the boat. Yelling "*Abwärts*!" they slid downward, hands around the vertical bars of the ladder to the combat center, and were immediately pulled away by their fellow sailors to make room for the man coming behind.

"Alarm! Diving!" sounded over the intercom through the boat, followed by an ear-piercing noise of ringing bells. Like bees in a disturbed hive the crew ran to their diving stations. With practiced speed they stopped the diesel engines, turned on the electromotors, closed the exhaust valves, and opened the top valves of the diving tanks. Its hydroplanes turned, the boat's bow went down. Brinker was the last to jump into the submerging boat. He closed the hatch firmly and secured it. Seconds later the sub was under water. Calmness returned.

"To fifty meters!" Brinker ordered.

"To fifty meters," repeated Helms, the first watch officer in charge of the two sailors at the hydroplanes. He stood with his body slightly bent to avoid banging his head against the pipes overhead.

Silence. Only the soft humming of the electromotors vibrated through the boat. Everyone watched Brinker, waiting for the next order. At this moment, skipper and crew were a single organism, every sense on alert.

"This is only a test dive," Brinker said over the intercom to reduce his men's tension. "We'll check the trim after taking on cargo."

Brinker spoke briefly to his chief engineer. Lieutenant Topper knew every nut, bolt and valve on the submarine intimately. To make the submarine neutrally buoyant, he had his machinists pump sea water out of the ballast tanks. To control the trim of the boat, water was pumped from the bow trim tanks to the aft tanks. Amounts of ballast were checked until the U-boat could be kept at the same depth without use of hydroplanes.

Brinker thought about the six SS officers who had come on board in Hardanger Fjord. They were housed in the bow torpedo room. He hoped they had some knowledge of U-boats so they wouldn't move around and mess up the trim.

"Boat is neutrally buoyant," Topper finally reported to the skipper.

"*Danke*," Brinker said. "Slowest speed forward!"

There was complete silence. Even the hum of the electromotors ceased. The sub prowled through the water.

Brinker turned to the petty officer in the listening room. "Check the sounding equipment. Can you still hear the big ships?"

"Yes, sir. At 210. No other targets audible."

"Good." He bent over the microphone. "Check for leaks!"

Reports soon came back from each compartment: "Everything watertight."

Brinker nodded. The boat was again in perfect diving

condition. "To periscope depth!"

Five minutes later he slid up the periscope and scanned the horizon. It was dark. Only the western horizon showed a silvery glow. "Everything clear," he said to the second watch officer at his side. "Take over the watch. Course is 295."

Now he had time to read the secret document given him by *Kapitän* Bauer, who had briefly spoken to the SS officers on the bow of the submarine. He picked up a mug of hot coffee and went to his office nook. Folding the table plate down, he opened his safe. As he pulled out the envelope, he remembered Bauer's words, when the two naval officers were alone for a short moment: "I wish you courage and good luck. Your assignment demands subtle intuition, perseverance and firm decisions. I don't know the details of your operation order, but I'm afraid it won't be easy with your strange guests. Stay firm and remember *you* are the commander of your boat. *You* are responsible for the success of this mission. Have a good trip. *Auf Wiedersehen!*"

Brinker picked up "*OPERATION FEUER ALARM* - Order No.2," opened it and read:

" .... The boat will be sailed to Quadrant AK 5587, southwest of Iceland. Any contact with enemy forces must be avoided. Under *no* circumstances, even in most favorable conditions, is an attack on hostile ships allowed. The boat has a single mission: to transport the containers under safest conditions to the location of deployment. Information about the content of the containers and the deployment will be provided at a later time. Any radio communication is forbidden. Repeat: absolutely forbidden."

What followed were instructions regarding the six SS officers.

"... *Kapitänleutnant* Brinker is responsible for the safety of the U-boat. However, he has no authority over the group of SS officers under the order of SS *Standartenführer* Krantz, the only officer authorized to direct the use of the containers. The crew of the submarine is not allowed to touch, open or investigate the equipment, parts or elements of the containers and/or their contents.

Stf. Krantz has authority to work in the forward torpedo room without the presence of crew members — if necessary. Crew members must abandon the space until allowed back by the SS officer in charge.

All contact between the U-boat commander and SS officers on board shall be conducted through *Stf.* Krantz.

Further orders will be provided after arrival in Quadrant AK 5587 by *Stf.* Krantz."

Stunned, Brinker read the signature of a certain SS *Standartenführer* Schmeltzer and a barely legible one — Bonnan or something similar. In the left corner of the sheet was the signature of *BdU*, Admiral Godt, the commander-in-chief of U-boats.

Now he became angry. Never had such a thing happened in the *Kriegsmarine*! Why did he not have the full information about the purpose of this patrol? He was being treated like a taxi driver. What was going on in Berlin? An order prepared by some top SS brass in Berlin for a U-boat *Kommandant*! Had the Nazi party taken over the *Kriegsmarine*?

Until now, he'd obeyed all orders from the *BdU*, even when he thought they were senseless. Others had told him stories of U-boats lost because of instructions based on faulty assumptions. Good times for the U-boats had ended in 1942 when American aircraft carriers and planes came to the Atlantic. Since then German U-boats had lost their efficiency and suffered tremendous losses. Now, it seemed the *Kriegsmarine* had been taken over by the Nazis...the damn Nazis who started the war that was destroying the country.

His fury grew. Should he turn the boat around and return to Wilhelmshaven? Or to Bergen in Norway? Would this be mutiny? He looked again at the order and saw the *BdU* 's signature. Had *Kapitän* Bauer actually read the order?

His fingers beat a staccato on the table. He needed to talk to Krantz. He weighed the question of protocol. Should he go to Krantz or should Krantz come to him? There was no room on the submarine where he could speak to Krantz alone. The

torpedo room was filled with crew members, the officers'
wardroom always occupied by off-duty officers. The skipper
decided he as *Kommandant* must be near the combat center at all
times. Krantz would have to meet him in the wardroom.

He needed a liaison to Krantz. The first watch officer had
many other responsibilities. The second watch officer, Lieutenant
Schroeder, had been in his crew for only two patrols. His
engineering officer, Lt. Topper, had his hands full on the seven
year old boat. The boat was four years on patrols in the Atlantic
and required many repairs. Topper should not be burdened with
another activity. The skipper felt he should have complete trust
in the liaison officer. His executive officer seemed to be the only
man for this job. He always remained in control. Yes, Helms
was just the man, the only officer he had on board during all ten
missions. Brinker trusted him completely.

He called Helms and instructed him to bring *Standartenführer*
Krantz to the officers' room. The SS officer appeared
immediately. When they were seated, the skipper asked Krantz,
"Are you adjusting to life on board?"

"Somewhat. We have established ourselves in the bow room.
However, we don't have enough beds. I must have three
additional beds."

"Did you have an opportunity to get any training at the U-boat
school before coming aboard?" Brinker asked.

"No. For staff officers there is no need for this."

"But at school you would have learned how small a submarine
is."

"We are staff officers and need our own beds. If there aren't
any on board, they must be built for us. Furthermore, the space
in the bow room is too narrow. We need more space!"

Brinker braced himself. "Apparently you aren't familiar with
a Type IX U-boat." He tried to speak in measured tones.
"Lieutenant Helms is the man responsible for seaworthiness of
the boat, so I suggest he show you around. You will see the
limitations of a submarine combat vessel. He is at your disposal
at any time."

"Four of my men could go immediately," Krantz said. "According to our instructions, one must stay in the bow room. That officer can make the tour later." Krantz stood up and moved to the bow room.

Helms looked at Brinker inquiringly.

"Explain the boat to them," Brinker instructed. "Treat them like people who've never been on a submarine. You can see they have no idea what we're all about."

Helms got up and followed Krantz to the bow room.

Brinker was worried. What could he expect from these men in the future?

7. Hardanger Fjord - April 3, 1945.

"I need to use your radio. Quick, where is it?" Svensen said.

Aboard the BIRGIT, Captain Per Ulfung, a huge, broad-shouldered man, shook his head. "Sorry, Major Svensen, we threw it overboard. If the Germans had caught us with it, we would have been killed. Before we reached the spit to pick you up, we were stopped and searched twice. They even poked their goddamn noses in the hold."

Erik rapidly reviewed his options. "Where's the nearest radio? Anything closer than Bergen? I sent Olaf overland, but he either didn't reach Bergen or something else happened."

"A fire," Per said. The blond beard covering half his face gave him the look of a Viking. "Two days ago the Germans discovered the building we sent messages from. They burned it to the ground. They arrested two of our men and are looking for the rest. There's no longer a radio in Bergen."

"My God! The Germans loaded ten cylinders from that damn factory onto a U-boat and I can't find a radio!" he yelled, venting his frustration on the BIRGIT's captain.

"Easy, man, easy," Per said. "You actually saw them loading cylinders from the factory? What's in the cylinders?"

"How the hell should I know? Listen, I'm sorry," Erik smiled at the captain. "I'm cold and hungry. I didn't mean to take it out on you. I just want to know how to communicate with Bath."

Per scrubbed at his beard with rough fisherman's hands, the knuckles cut and swollen, skin chapped. His gray turtleneck sweater and dark pants, stuffed into knee-high boots, were smeared with fish scales and blood. A strong odor of fish had bombarded Erik's nose the minute he'd boarded the boat. If Per Ulfung and his crew were not real fishermen, they had certainly made themselves and their boat look and smell real enough.

"Tell you what," the captain said. "How about Scotland? We can put you off at Aberdeen if our fuel holds out."

"Aberdeen? God dammit! I have to get a report to OSS. I

wasn't planning to deliver it in person. Are you telling me Aberdeen's the nearest radio?" Frustrated, Erik peeled off his camouflage suit and stuffed it into his knapsack.

Per spread his hands in a gesture of resignation. "It's the best I can do and I'm not even sure we've enough fuel to do that."

Aberdeen? The sub could be to hell and gone by then. Erik stared at the captain. Up to now, he'd known Per as an experienced resistance fighter. Per knew what was going on in MILORG, the Norwegian underground. It was Per who transported Olaf to the spit in Hardanger Fjord, who returned at intervals to replenish his supplies. Why hadn't Olaf known about the burned building in Bergen? Of course, if they were all losing their damn radios it was a wonder any of them knew anything. He decided he would have to trust the captain.

"How far away is the sub?" Erik asked. "Is it heading north or south toward Germany?"

"That's a good question." Per stepped to the wheelhouse. "Sven, bring us up to where we can see that convoy we passed." Opening a lunch box, he handed Erik a sandwich. "Eat while you have the chance. I'm going below to check the fuel gauge."

Erik wolfed down the bread and cheese. God, a beer sure would taste good now!

Per returned a moment later, his face serious. "I talked with Gunnar, the engineer. If we travel at no more than six knots we might make Aberdeen on what fuel we have. Of course, it'll depend on the wind and the tides. I can't guarantee we'll get you there."

Erik frowned. "What if we run out of fuel in mid-ocean?"

Per shrugged. "Then we wait for someone to rescue us."

"Just like that?"

"You want a radio, don't you?"

"Cap'n!" called the sailor on the bow. "Convoy to starboard!"

Erik followed Per to the bow. He swung his glasses to his eyes and scanned the horizon. Nothing. He swept the area again. There! Black specks, barely visible on the silvery horizon.

"The convoy's heading north," Per stated.

"It's Aberdeen then," Erik replied. "As fast as you can go on the fuel you have. Every hour we lose will make it that much harder for our planes to find the U-boat."

"Captain!" yelled the sailor at the stern. "German fast torpedo boats starboard!"

"I'll go below," Erik said.

"Stay where you are," Per warned. "If they see you running below deck, it will rouse their curiosity. Let me do all the talking. Your Norwegian has too much American in it."

Three German boats bore down on the BIRGIT, their searchlights bathing the hull and the wheelhouse in a bright glare. One boat came alongside. Three young Germans jumped onto the BIRGIT's deck. Moving quickly across, they looked into each corner. Erik felt exposed, on center stage. His face stiff, his knees locked, he fought against an overpowering desire to go below. Thank God he had taken off his camouflage fatigues! In his sweater and pants he didn't look that different from Per and his crew. Two Germans passed Erik, went to the stern and looked into the wheelhouse. The third studied each face of the BIRGIT's crew. Erik felt his cheeks flushing when the sailor stared at him for seconds that seemed minutes to Erik. The officer of the motorboat whistled. The sailor returned to Erik and looked at him again as if he'd seen something strange. Was he suspicious? Erik felt naked. The sailor looked for his comrades. Another whistle and the two Germans jumped back to their fast boat. The third sailor followed them.

Their boats circled the BIRGIT once more. Then, just as suddenly as they had appeared, they sped away.

"Thank God," Per sighed. "I just remembered the clothes you took off and put in your knapsack. We're lucky they didn't turn everything upside down as in the first search."

"Does this happen often?" Erik asked.

Per grinned. "Sure, and it never gets any easier. You attached to MI-5?"

"No, to OSS, *American* Intelligence. We cooperate with the British."

"Been at it long?"

"Two years."

"Me too."

"You ever been to Aberdeen?" Erik asked.

"Two years ago. My first assignment. I picked up some Norwegian agents who later blew up three German ships. I tell you, that makes it all worthwhile."

"Your people did a damn good job in Ryukan when they cracked the Norsk Hydro Plant."

"Yes, but there were reprisals. Would you believe our daily rations are only eight hundred calories now? Not even a child can live on that. If we don't rid ourselves of the Germans soon, we'll all starve to death." Erik remembered the bread and cheese he had eaten so hungrily. Had it been Per's dinner?

The captain went to the deck house. Erik heard him ordering Bjorn, his mate, to maintain a speed of six knots. Bjorn, gray-haired with a pleasant face and ready smile, nodded and took the helm.

Suddenly tired, Erik stumbled down the ladder and stretched out on an empty bunk.

The captain followed him. "Listen, before you go to sleep, I heard earlier this week that our people in Oslo got a look at one of the trucks going to the factory at Hardanger. It was loaded with boxes from a German chemical company. The boxes were stamped *OPERATION FEUER ALARM* and *GIFTIG!* Our men couldn't get close enough to look inside."

"Thanks," Erik said, frowning. *GIFTIG* - Poisonous? What the hell was going on in that factory? "If we make it with the fuel we have, when will we reach Aberdeen?" he asked.

"Tomorrow afternoon."

Erik turned his face to the bulkhead, an arm over his eyes. Damn! Another 18 hours or more before he could reach a radio. He listened to the steady throbbing of the boat's engine, eating up fuel, and realized there was a good chance they wouldn't make Aberdeen at all. The U-boat had every chance to slip away on its unknown mission. His trip to the fjord had been in vain.

8. North Atlantic - April 4, 1945.

Lieutenant Helms was well aware of his skipper's desire to knock some sense into their uninvited guests. From what he had seen, the SS officers were not likely to be cooperative. However, he greeted them in the bow torpedo room with calm formality and began the tour.

"Those tubes. They're loaded with torpedoes. We call them 'eels.' *Torpedomaat* Tenner is in charge. Tenner and his men are the only ones allowed to touch any of the valves, levers and buttons. It's hazardous for others to touch them."

Helms stared at Krantz who, not accustomed to a rolling submarine, was having trouble standing erect on the deck of the smoothly moving boat. The other five landlubbers did better at steadying themselves.

"Playing with the torpedo tubes could mean death for us all. The eels are sharp ammunition. Below the table and the deck plates are more eels to be used for reloading. See them there?" He pointed below the long tables.

"They don't look so dangerous," Krantz sneered.

"Dangerous enough. They sink the ship they hit."

"I don't want them here," Krantz said.

How ignorant these men are! Helms thought. But he answered calmly, "We'll look for space as we go through the other rooms."

Stepping to a post with a small mirror, he opened a miniature fold-out basin. "This is the washing facility for the crew. Each day we use one cup of drinking water per person. Otherwise, we don't have enough sweet water for everyone on board."

Krantz stood in front of the unfolded basin and quickly looked into the mirror. "I need more water to shave." His right hand stroked his forehead where he had a badly healed scar on the right side. Then his face darkened as he stroked the black stubbles on his cheeks.

"Sweet water is for brushing our teeth," Helms said.

"Where are the shower rooms and bath tubs?" one SS officer asked. "Can we take a bath on Saturdays?"

How stupid can you get? Helms thought. But he controlled himself and said, "There are none."

The officers looked stunned, disbelief on their faces.

"Two weeks after leaving port, everyone gets one bucket of water for bathing," Helms continued. "We do that here in the torpedo room. One at a time. We undress and wash the whole body."

Helms turned to the end of the long room. "This is a bulkhead separating the pressure hull of the boat into water-tight sections."

With long-practiced speed he squeezed himself through the small round opening, three feet in diameter. Slowly and awkwardly the SS men followed him, struggling hard to get through. Krantz ordered one of his men to stay in the torpedo room. Then he stood in front of the round opening, reluctant to bow down, step through with one leg and pull his body into the other room. Helms saw how much effort it cost the SS officer to do this.

Their next stop was a long narrow room with berths on both sides, two long tables and benches in the middle. Off-duty crew members read, played cards, wrote letters or just simply lay on their bunks. Smoked hams, sausages and hammocks with bread loaves or vegetables hung from hooks in the overhead. Covering the entire overhead, they swung uniformly from side to side as the U-boat rolled. The lamplight created spooky images as it shone downward over the moving objects. Every inch of the deck was used to store cans and nets with salamis, cookie packages, flour bags, large cheese discs and various other food stuffs. The little bit of space left was just enough for the sailors to sit at the table with their legs spread wide apart, because below the table food was packed tightly.

"We're in the crew's quarters," Helms explained. "Engine personnel, radiomen, soundmen and specialists, all crowded together here. It's the same as in the torpedo room. Two men per berth on our boat, enlisted men as well as officers. Those off-duty take turns at the bunks with their on-duty partners. The only people with their own beds are the *Kommandant* and the chief engineer. Since they don't have fixed watches, they are on duty day and night and need their own beds. I share my bunk with the second watch officer."

The SS men exchanged looks.

Ignoring the appalled expressions on the faces of the little group, Helms ushered them through the petty officers' quarters to the galley. They pushed against each other to see the small room. The cook in a white shirt and pants turned his upper body between a shiny and sparkling stainless steel range and a narrow counter, cutting up meat and vegetables. Four large pots stood on the electric plates of the range. Only an occasional foot movement altered the cook's stance, the space was so small.

The cook pointed with his knife to the raised bars around the range. "To keep the pots in place when the boat rolls and pitches," he explained. "Behind you is the fridge."

The SS men turned around. One of them opened the door and peered into the opening. The fridge was filled to the last cubic inch. Cold air flowed out like a miniature waterfall. He quickly closed the door.

"At the side of the fridge is the second toilet." The cook pointed. "We can't use it now, because it's filled with cans, potatoes, vegetables, butter and coffee." He nodded at a large bowl: "Prunes in this bowl at all times. You'll need them soon to get your bowels in order. We don't get enough exercise. You'll learn what it means in the next few days."

A blond SS officer with a round face and a pot-belly asked: "Where is the kitchen for us, the officers?"

"There's only one galley," Helms replied. "We all eat the same food, the *Kommandant* included." He motioned the group to move on. "We'll pass now through the wardroom."

Krantz turned to him. "We're staff personnel from the Superior SS Planning Staff. We demand a special kitchen. I'll speak to the *Kommandant* about this."

Helms ignored him.

"We need also a few men to polish our boots and brush our uniforms," the SS officer with a Hitler-moustache said. "They get very dirty on this damned boat." He turned to Helms, frowning at the officer's brown jacket and pants. "By the way, why don't you wear your blue uniform?"

Helms suppressed a smile. "We wear them only on shore. Here on the boat we wear the brown." Grinning, he pointed to his outfit. "They used to be British uniforms. Our army found them in France during the occupation. The British left them in storage when they fled Dunkirk. Admiral Dönitz found them more practical than our old outfits. He confiscated them for the submariners."

The red-haired officer asked, "Why doesn't the commander wear his blue uniform with the gold stripes on the sleeves to show his rank?"

Helms marveled at how infatuated they seemed with uniforms. He said, "Our skipper — that's what we call him — our skipper wears the same uniform as we do. You can only tell him from the rest of us by his white cap cover."

"Everything looks so non-military," Krantz objected. "When do you have roll calls, inspections and political appeals?"

"Never at sea," the first watch officer replied. "When we return from patrol we're greeted briefly by our flotilla commander. Then we leave for home furlough. There aren't any political appeals for us. We're just sailors."

The red-haired officer cleared his throat. "How come the sailors on board never salute us when they pass by? Why don't they raise their arms in the national salute?"

"Space on a U-boat is so limited it would be impractical to salute," Helms answered patiently. "We wouldn't be able to work well if everyone raised his arm when passing a superior."

"But how can you have authority when you don't enforce saluting?" Krantz insisted.

"You'll understand that when we have contact with the enemy," Helms said. "Our skipper is fully in control and everybody does the job he is trained for. You'll now see the radio shack and the listening room."

In the radio room two of the SS men studied the equipment thoroughly. "Where's the transmitter?" the officer with the Hitler moustache asked.

The radio operator pushed up one side of his earphones and pointed with his hand to a panel with numerous dials and buttons.

"How far can you reach with it?" the SS man asked.

"To any point of the world."

"And this is?"

"The receiver." The radio operator turned a knob. Jazz filled the room. "From Ottawa, Canada."

"Phooey! Degenerate noise of frogs! Can't you get German march music?" the SS officer asked. "Hey, don't you know it's forbidden to listen to enemy stations?"

"I have to know what the enemy's doing in the Atlantic. It's mandatory we hear that. Even though they lie as much as Goebbels."

"Listen, man, are you a defeatist?" one officer demanded.

"I'm on my ninth U-boat patrol. I can't be a defeatist. I'm here doing my duty." The radioman put his earphone back on and busied himself with his equipment.

The SS men turned toward the listening room. "Rotten bunch of hooligans, all of them!" the tall SS officer whispered to his boss.

Helms heard it and his brows knit in anger.

Krantz demanded of the soundman, "What can you hear with this device?"

"When underwater, I can hear propeller and engine noises. And I can determine the direction by moving this wheel. It's important to monitor destroyers when they're chasing us. What I hear and report helps the skipper decide on appropriate evasion maneuvers."

Helms put a finger to his lips as they passed through the officers' wardroom where off-duty officers slept in their bunks. Here was the same narrow space with barely enough room to walk through, the cans and packages stowed in every corner, the sausages and hammocks swinging from the ceiling.

Helms stopped in the control room. When the five officers caught up, he continued his lecture: "Underwater, the boat is controlled from here. Only authorized personnel go to the upper combat center and the conning tower. Here are the periscopes and the gyro-compass."

"Why are there so many pipes and valves?" Krantz asked.

"From here the chief engineer uses all the equipment needed for diving, trimming and ballasting the boat."

The SS officers stared at the array of valves and pipes in wonder. Krantz asked, "Who can tell the valves apart?"

"The chief engineer and his assistants. Next we have the engine room. The diesel engines are so noisy we won't be able to hear each other. Walk through quickly." He opened the round hatch of the bulkhead, squeezed through, went the length of the room and turned at the other end to observe the SS men.

They covered their ears with their hands. Two steps into the room, they brought their hands to their cheeks for protection against the unexpected heat. The smell of diesel oil and exhaust gases made them wrinkle their noses. A few more steps and the men passed below a ventilator conduit where fresh, cool air blew against them, tousling their hair.

One step farther they were in a hot zone again. Machinists, their ears covered by insulator caps, grinned and waved in a friendly manner. Next they passed between a pair of 2,200 HP diesel engines with dozens of levers and springs moving up and down. The engine noise was unbelievable. The SS men stopped when they sensed the heat of the engines and didn't know how to keep their balance between the hot diesel motors without reaching out and burning their hands. Finally, they grabbed the hand rails and walked through the narrow space.

After the noisy diesels, they passed between the cool electromotors into the rear torpedo room, where they tried to brush the dust from their black uniforms. Krantz became angry when the SS officer with the Hitler-moustache showed him an oil stain on his swastika band. It must have brushed on one of the many pipes.

"Damned oily, this boat! Can't they keep it clean?"

"This is the second-most important room, the boat's toilet," Helms explained. "Right now it's unoccupied. In three or four days, people line up here."

"Because of the prunes?" the red-haired officer asked. "I don't like prunes."

"You will. Because we stand, sit or sleep the whole time, walking to the toilet is the only daily exercise. You will be glad of the help from the prunes." He pointed to the torpedo tube, "This is our aft torpedo room."

Krantz seemed surprised. "This is the whole boat?"

"Where is the bar?" another SS man asked, half joking.

Helms smiled maliciously. "No bar on board. No smoking, no beer, no *schnapps* on a submarine."

"No women either?" The tallest officer asked with a grin until a look from Krantz warned him.

Leading them back through the boat, Helms pointed out the fifty crew members' tasks and their combat stations. The SS men listened attentively.

"One could get claustrophobia here!" one SS man said. "How long have you been on this boat?" he asked.

"Four years with the U-boat service. Ten patrols on this boat."

"That's a long time," Krantz said.

"I couldn't stand that," another officer said.

"How can you damned Prussians live on such a small boat?" an SS officer asked in his Bavarian dialect.

"Where is the room for storing our kit bags? I didn't see any," Krantz complained.

As if on cue, they all began talking. "I didn't see any material to build beds... Where is the bunker for the U-boat *Kommandant*?... His own room?... Where is a hall for political rallies?... Where are your machine guns and pistols?"

Helms was amused. "Please, gentlemen. I've shown you the entire boat. We don't have guns and pistols. We sink ships with torpedoes. The skipper has no own room. He has a small desk he unfolds in the officers' wardroom. That's his office cubicle. During an underwater attack our commander is in the combat center. When we surface he directs the battle from the conning tower." He stopped for a moment. "We all live together and if we're hit, we all share the same fate."

Krantz looked at Helms. "The tour of the boat was informative. It's a tough life on a U-boat." He straightened his black jacket. "Now I want to see the commander."

"Certainly." Surprised, Helms saw a deep anger in Krantz's face.

Kapitänleutnant Brinker sat at his small unfolded table in the wardroom writing in his log book. Helms appeared with the five SS officers in tow. "Grand tour through the boat is finished," Helms reported.

"*Danke*," the skipper said, then turned to Krantz. "How did you like our boat? A nice cruise ship, isn't it?"

"I'm impressed by its small size," Krantz said, still trying to keep himself erect on the rolling boat. "Space really is limited. I didn't know that. We'll have to adjust to it. I present my staff officers to you, *Herr Kapitänleutnant*." He pointed to the blond, smart-looking officer, who clicked his heels and stood at attention. "SS Lieutenant Colonel Steltner, my assistant."

Steltner raised his arm in the Nazi salute, looking into the skipper's eyes. He almost fell as the boat rolled. He quickly lowered his arm to hold on to the bunk on his right.

Brinker smiled, stepped to him and shook his hand.

Steltner raised his hand again briefly, then stepped back to lean against the table.

Krantz pointed to the thin, red-haired man, who clicked his heels and raised his arm, his hand knocking against a pipe. Startled, he jerked his arm back.

"SS Major Schmidt."

Pointing to the officer with the Hitler-moustache, Krantz said, "SS Major Tauber."

Tauber's raised hand knocked down a thick Bologna sausage which hung from the overhead. Brinker smiled as Tauber bent to pick it up. Calmly, Helms replaced it on its hook over their heads.

Brinker stepped forward and shook hands with both officers.

Krantz then said, "SS Lieutenant Radke."

Brinker shook hands with the tall SS officer who had difficulty holding his head between the swinging sausages.

"I hope you will feel well on the boat," Brinker said to the officers. "I'm sure in a few days you'll become real seamen."

"Would you advise us," Krantz said, "on how we can assist you?"

"Thank you for your offer. Since you haven't attended U-boat school, it would be difficult to train you now. But I will explain your activities during diving and combat. During diving maneuvers, you are not to leave the bow room or move around. Otherwise it will change the trim and could endanger the boat, even sink it. The same rule applies in a combat situation. You must stay in your room and care for the equipment you brought aboard. Make sure everything is well tied down."

Obviously, Krantz was not ready to accept Brinker's rules without a comment. "There will be *no* combat situations. It will be your duty to avoid any contact with the enemy," he said firmly, holding onto the bunk at his left. "Understand? It would be a catastrophe for our mission."

Brinker said, "Due to our new operation order, I'll not attack. However, if we're discovered by our enemies they won't go by Berlin's rules. They'll simply try to destroy us."

For several moments Krantz stared at the empty table. Then, with a motion of his hand, he dismissed his four officers. They stretched their bodies stiffly, raised their arms and left the room.

"Where is your march order?" Krantz asked.

The skipper took the order from his safe and spread it on the table. He went over each point with the SS officer.

Krantz's most urgent concern was with the narrow space in the bow torpedo room — the only spot he had been assigned by

Führer Headquarters for his people, crates and kit bags.

"Again, I demand three more beds. We're staff personnel and have to sleep in our own beds."

"Sorry, that's impossible," the skipper said. "I let six crew members off in Hardanger Fjord. You got their three bunks. As *Kapitän* Bauer explained to you, the bunks must be shared."

"I didn't understand his remark. This is impossible! Each of us must have his own bed. That is imperative."

"As you've seen, there are no additional bunks on the boat. Your SS staff in Berlin obviously accepted this."

"I demand three of your sailors sleep on the floor."

"You mean six because they share their three bunks with each other."

"*Ja!*"

"Never! My officers and petty officers share their bunks. So will yours. And the sailors and machinists have strenuous duty, twelve hours each day. No weekends off. If they are tired when on duty, one mistake could sink our boat. All deck space must be used for easy passage."

Krantz swallowed twice. "I want to hear from you where we can stow our belongings."

Brinker said: "You're now using the space we need for the torpedo handling. I suggest you get rid of all unnecessary items." Opening the door of his small closet he pointed to the few sweaters, pants and underwear, all neatly folded. "That's all I have. Throw your boots, uniforms and coats overboard. Keep just your work clothes, as we do."

Shock plainly showed on Krantz's face. "This is an insult! Our uniforms are special to us, a commitment to the *Führer*. I can never get rid of my uniform."

Brinker winced. "Think twice about it. There isn't any more space. Six days and we'll be in the target area."

Krantz got up and stalked from the room.

For a long time Brinker sat in thought. The presence of the SS officers would be a great irritant to his crew, and if the arrogant bastards didn't adjust, it could mean the end of them all.

9. North Sea - April 6, 1945.

At dawn Erik Svensen woke, not sure where he was. It took him a few moments to remember he was aboard the rolling BIRGIT, sailing to Aberdeen, Scotland. He lay with closed eyes, listening to the monotonous sounds of the diesel engine. Per, the boat's captain, jumped from the other bunk and went up on deck. Erik got up and slowly followed, but stayed below on the steps, his head in the open door. There seemed to be no horizon between the gray sea and the cloud-covered sky. It was all one continuous bleak color.

Erik stepped up on deck to greet Per and Sven.

"We are more than halfway to Aberdeen!" Per reported. "Unfortunately, the morning breeze comes from the west. It's slowing down the boat. We aren't doing more than five knots." He offered Erik a cup of coffee. "Or what passes for coffee these days," Per said.

Erik made a face, but swallowed the hot brew anyway. "Can't we go faster?" he asked.

"Sorry. We'd be using extra fuel."

Erik sipped at his coffee and studied the boat. The bolts holding the shrouds were rusty. Long brownish streaks ran over wooden timbers that had splintered in various parts. It didn't look as though the boat had been painted for at least four years. From the stuttering of the diesel engine he could tell it needed an overhaul too. Erik wrinkled his nose. The smell of fish from the cargo room mingled with the odor of the diesel fuel.

"How much fishing do you really do?" he asked.

"Not much. We work full time for the resistance and use our fishing gear only as cover."

"Who pays you?"

"MILORG, the resistance."

"And your family? Who takes care of them?"

"MILORG. My wife's working and the kids are helping as messengers. Are you married?"

"I was. My wife was shot by the Nazis in Trondheim." Erik felt a familiar stab in his stomach. The death of his wife had changed his life completely. He had volunteered immediately to work with MI-5 in Canada. To work against the Nazis and take his revenge. His marriage was a very happy one because both partners worked hard to understand each other's needs.

"Sorry. What was an American woman doing in Trondheim?" Per asked.

"Just visiting her sick mother."

"Any children?"

"A boy of twelve. Harald is his name."

"He's in America?"

"Yes. In San Francisco." Erik thought of the long separation from his son which was his most serious problem. When could he have Harald again in his arms? It wasn't enough to write a letter every two weeks. Erik had never assumed the war would stretch over six years.

"You've been in Trondheim?"

"No. But I hope to get there soon." Erik stared into the water. "That's why I joined the OSS. When my wife visited her mother, some SS car was blown up by Norwegian resistance fighters. To avenge this act, the SS troops drove through the city and fired randomly at persons on the streets. My wife was one of eighty people killed. I immediately joined the OSS. That's the reason why my son is alone in California." He drank some coffee, tossed the rest of it into the opaque sea, and swallowed the bile in his throat. "I'm the world's prize fool."

"No, no," Per insisted. "We all have our dreams. Hang on to yours. This war can't last forever. When did you come to Norway?"

"Two days ago. By parachute."

"From where?"

"Bath, England. The OSS works there with MI-5."

"I know." Per pointed at the ocean which had suddenly calmed. "I'll have Gunnar check the fuel again." He stepped over to the hatch of the diesel room and whistled.

Gunnar's bald head appeared. What was left of his hair had been neatly combed up toward his forehead.

"Check the fuel," Erik heard Per say. "Can we make it faster?"

After a while Gunnar appeared in the door. "There's only enough fuel for about six hours."

Erik winced. "Six more hours?"

Per returned to the steering house and bent over the nautical chart. "I'm still not sure we can make it."

"Goddamn! We'd better start looking for British fishing vessels in the area. Something with a radio!" He took the binoculars and scanned the horizon.

Per came to stand beside him. "The wind's veering, almost out of the east. I've got an old sail I could try, but I doubt it's any good. Too old. It could rip apart any time." He turned to Jens, the nearest sailor. "Let's try it anyway. Hoist it."

Jens went to the bow and pulled out a triangular, brown sail from the storage box. He clamped it to the bow wire and hoisted it.

Erik held his breath as the breeze caught the piece of canvas. It held. Half an hour later, the wind was a steady breeze from behind, pushing the boat westward. Will we make it? Erik thought. What if not?

Still watching for other vessels, Erik guessed their speed at eight knots. He hummed a song he had sung when he was thirteen years old, using the ferry from Coronado to attend school in San Diego. A golden time without problems. But now?! A few spots of blue sky appeared among the gray clouds.

Erik thought that the full-blown sail looked like the puffed-out cheeks of an inspired trumpet player. He drank the hot liquid and bent over the charts, looking for the Norwegian fjords where agents worked on intelligence assignments. If he only knew what was in the cylinders loaded on the U-boat! Where would it be right now?

A ripping noise brought his head up from the charts. The sail! It broke into several small pieces and flapped in the wind like a shredded flag on a pole!

"I was afraid it wouldn't last," Per said. "But we'll leave it there. It still pulls us forward."

Erik could do nothing else but take up his binoculars and once again scan the horizon covered by a colorless wall of thin fog. He estimated visibility to be two to three miles.

Per suggested they eat lunch. Everybody chewed a dry sandwich without saying a word. The diesel noise became intermittent.

"What's happening to our diesel?" Erik asked Per.

"Maybe we're running out of fuel."

The engine stopped. The last drop of fuel had been used. The BIRGIT drifted toward Scotland, pulled by its noisily flapping pieces of canvas.

"What do we do now?" Erik asked.

"Drift to Scotland."

Erik almost panicked. How many hours are we losing now? Can the wind turn around and move us back to Norway? Is everything in vain? He didn't put the binoculars down. In the middle of the afternoon Erik finally saw something. "Aren't there two boats, portside?" he yelled to Per.

Per stepped out of the steering house and looked through his own binoculars. "Right! We made it!"

"Can they be German?" Erik asked.

"No. Impossible. We are too close to Scotland. They look like typical British boats. Now you'll have your radio."

"Will they see us?"

"Just like we see them. Don't worry. They're not going to pass up a strange craft in these waters and that damn sail is plenty strange enough. We'll have visitors soon."

Forty minutes later the first boat moved alongside. Its rusty hull looked to be in worse shape than the BIRGIT. The English — or were they Scots? — on the rusty deck studied the BIRGIT and its crew with suspicion.

"What's up?" one of them called over.

"We need help," Per called back. "We're out of fuel. We're

from Bergen on our way to Aberdeen. Can you tow us?"

"We'll have to inspect your boat first," the British captain
called. A sailor threw a line over to Jens who tied it around a
bollard. The British captain and one of his men, both in dirty,
reddish overalls, jumped to BIRGIT's deck. Without any
greeting, the captain walked to the bow, looked into the storage
nook, turned around, looked down into the cargo space, and
finally entered the diesel room.

Gunnar showed him the fuel gauge. The captain scanned the
room and knocked his fist against the fuel tank. It reverberated
emptily. Still not convinced of the Norwegian boat's innocence,
he returned to the deck and the stern, checked the mast and the
torn sail. He pointed to an oar and said to his sailor: "Stir up
that heap of smelly fish in the cargo room. Anything hidden
there?"

Several times the young man poked the oar down to the
bottom, his face puckered as he tried not to breathe.

"All right," the British captain finally said. "I just had to make
sure you aren't a German floating bomb."

Erik stepped forward impatiently. "I'm Major Erik Svensen
with American Intelligence. I need to use your radio. It's an
emergency." The captain, as tall as Erik, looked directly into
Erik's eyes and stroked the blond moustache that hid part of his
mouth. Then he turned to Per. "My name is Graeme, spelled the
Scottish way, not the British. You say you're from Bergen?"

Per answered: "Yes. I was in Aberdeen twice two years ago.
The harbour master should know my boat."

Graeme reflected, turned back to Erik and said, "You Yanks
are always in such a bloody hurry. We don't have a radio, but
I can give you a tow."

The full moon shone down on the jetties of Aberdeen harbor.
A strange tower like a smaller version of an airport's control
tower poked up through smaller buildings. Graeme maneuvered
the BIRGIT toward the pier to a steep ladder and pointed in the
direction of the nearby buildings. "The office of the harbour

master is over there."

Erik delayed only long enough to shake Per's and Graeme's hands, and then scrambled up the ladder to the quay and hurried to one of the old buildings near the tower.

Inside, a British lieutenant in his fifties, a reservist, and three older sailors sat in the harbour master's office. A clear light bulb on a cord dangled from the ceiling and lit up the room, which held two desks heaped with papers and folders.

Erik introduced himself and asked to be connected with MI-5, code number 24-301. The British lieutenant understood immediately. He led Erik through a long hallway to another room and closed the door behind them. Another three minutes and Erik was on the line with Colonel Bob Jones, his supervisor in the Bath office. He gave a swift account of his observations in the fjord.

"Only one sub?" Colonel Jones demanded. "Four freighters for a convoy? What damage can one sub do?"

"Not the sub as such, it's what they loaded onto the sub. I tell you, they had security around that factory so tight no one could get in. Those cylinders have to be important. They put six SS on board the U-boat."

Jones' silence was eloquent. When he spoke, he sounded tired, his voice harsh. "I'll see what I can do at this end. Better get to the Aberdeen airport as soon as you can. I'll try to find a plane for you."

Three hours later a military plane flew Erik to Bath Military Airport.

10. Northeast of Iceland - April 7, 1945.

SS *Standartenführer* Albert Krantz lay on his bunk in the torpedo room of U-888, his thin face shaved twice every day with one cup of water, revealing no sign of his inner rage.

He could not forget the embarrassing scene on the bow after boarding the U-boat. The way *Kapitän* Bauer had introduced him to *Kapitänleutnant* Brinker had been insufferable. Bauer had made it clear that the *Kommandant* of a U-boat was the only man responsible for the operation of a vessel of the *Kriegsmarine*, as if a lowly sailor could begin to rank with an SS colonel who worked directly under Himmler!

Another chagrin was the fact that he had been ordered to stay in the torpedo room. In Berlin, when he first received the assignment, he had dreamed of having his own staff room with an attached large meeting room where he could hold daily political rallies with the crew. Now, after touring the U-boat, he realized it had been a mistake not to take the training at the U-boat school.

It was all the fault of that fat pig, Schmeltzer. How could Himmler assign a "Nobody" like Schmeltzer to something as important as *OPERATION FEUER ALARM*?

Schmeltzer should have informed him about the limited capacities of a U-boat. And in ten days, when he would report the news of the successful deployment of the miracle weapon to the *Führer*, it would be that fat pig Schmeltzer who would get all the credit for the operation. Schmeltzer would be the person celebrated as the man who brought the Final Victory to the German nation.

An uncontrollable shudder shook Krantz. He would be far away. It would take weeks for him to appear in Germany. By then the only rewards would be the *Führer*'s handshake and a tap on the shoulder from Schmeltzer. Fat pig Schmeltzer would be promoted to SS *Brigadeführer*, a general's rank, and be a position above him.

Intolerable! Krantz wanted to scream it at the top of his lungs, but years of self-control kept him rigid and silent.

He had been faithful to the party. As a young storm trooper in the 1920s he had enjoyed bashing "Social Democrats" and "Commies" in nocturnal rallies. He gained a reputation for being tough, for being a loyal follower, one who loved beating and picking the political enemies of the National Socialist Party. Once he almost died. A young Social Democrat hit him with a shovel so hard he had been in the hospital for a month. While there, Hitler had taken him by the hand and thanked him for his devotion. He stroked the scar on his forehead.

A burst of laughter from the sailors in the torpedo room broke his concentration. He listened to what they were saying.

"I screwed her first on the bench in the park, then again in her bedroom. Twice!"

"Really? Is it true?"

"Believe me, she was stark naked and aroused like hell..."

Bah! More lies about their sexual prowess. Did all sailors speak so many lies?

He could tell them true stories that would arouse them instantly. He didn't need to lie about his erotic adventures in Spain, where he fought on General Franco's side with the German Legion Condor in the 1930s.

Too bad his wife, Lore, had grown so fat and dull. She was a useless cow, not even enough woman to bear him sons.

Ah, well, he had Gerda, his slender secretary, whenever he needed release. There was never any shortage of women for him, the rising star of the Party. Hadn't Himmler himself selected him for this assignment? Promoted him to colonel for his blood bath in Babi Yar when he was behind the front lines in the Ukraine? He had killed there more than 10,000 Jews.

Returning to the present, Krantz abandoned his memories. Instead, he began thinking of ways to strengthen his position on the U-boat. He was only in command of his five officers who had nothing to do. Why did Schmeltzer arrange for him to stay in the bow room? He couldn't stand this *Kommandant* who had

insulted him. He should throw his uniforms overboard! But he
still needed this *Kapitänleutnant* to sail him to the deployment
area. How could he take command of the boat? When was the
right moment?

11. North of Iceland - April 8, 1945.

U-888 steamed through the rough waters of the North Atlantic on a southwest course parallel to Greenland's coast. A howling gale of force 8 to 10 had developed over the last ten hours, typical for the region north of Iceland. The wind whipped up the water in a heaving turmoil of white-capped waves, 30 to 40 feet high, with 400 to 500 feet between crests. Brinker ordered a course directly into the waves. The U-boat rode up an approaching mountain of water, then sliced through the foaming breakers, the conning tower cutting through the turbulent water. The two officers, Helms and Hartmann, held in place by heavy leather and steel harnesses around their bodies, stood guard in the turret. The harnesses were hooked with four steel wires to eyelets welded to the conning tower. The slender body of the submarine broke through the towering wave crests. As the foamy water crashed over the turret, the two men lost their footing and were thrown to the floor. They struggled erect as the water drained from the turret's U-shaped enclosure. Then the sub flipped down from the top of the wave into a water valley, quivering heavily, to repeat the cycle, riding up the next wave.

Helms checked his harness. "*Scheisse*! I hope it doesn't break."

"Remember how we lost Wendel?"

"*Ja*. Poor fellow."

Hartmann had to close the turret hatch each time before the boat cut through the wave. He opened it again after the green water had run out of the conning tower tub. Curtains of spray above the breakers reduced visibility to less than a mile. Low clouds hovered over the submarine, releasing heavy rain from time to time. In such dense showers visibility was further diminished so that at times the men on the bridge could see barely 200 yards ahead of them. The loud, howling wind sounded like an airplane diving on them, but they knew no plane could fly in this weather. If a destroyer should suddenly appear,

the sub would have to dive immediately. And there would only
be enough time for the two officers to jump down into the boat
before the turbulent ocean closed over the conning tower. Cold
water seeped through the protective towels around their necks
and oozed down their backs.

"Why don't we submerge?" Hartmann yelled at Helms. "Even
if we saw the QUEEN MARY, we couldn't torpedo her."

"We have to get through this strait quickly. Too many Brits
here."

While Helms and Hartmann waited for their two-hour watch
to end, the SS men lay in their bunks, unable to do more than
groan. They were sea sick and couldn't eat. The smell of rich
food eaten by sailors in their room made them even sicker. They
threw up over and over again.

Yesterday Boatswain Hartmann had ordered the sailors to tie
three SS men to their bunks to keep them from falling out, the
other three to the bench at the table, and saw that the buckets
used by the officers were cleaned often. Looking after Krantz
now, Hartmann was shocked to see him half dead.

Eventually, the gale weakened and disappeared. The boat
returned to its usual rolling pitch. Life again became dull and
time dragged. The heavy weather had tired the crew. The men
were bored, always seeing the same faces, always performing the
same chores. They talked of food, looking forward eagerly to the
next meal. They read a book or letters from home again and
again or stared at the pin-up pictures glued to the doors of their
small lockers. Some told dirty jokes and bragged about their
sexual adventures during the last furlough. The noise from the
diesel engines and ventilators became monotonous. The swaying
motion of the left-over sausages and food-filled nets hanging
from the overhead slowly got on the nerves of the crew.

Then the food began to smell. The bread turned moldy. The
smell of the spicy salami sausages became intolerable.

"Damned shit!" shouted the chief engineer. "We need another
storm. This is the most dangerous place for us. Who sent us
through this narrow strait?"

The diesel machinists got tired of the routine of six hours on-duty, six off, six on, six off. They sometimes fell asleep of boredom in the engine room.

With the boat stable, the SS men felt better again. Sailors helped them to clean their mattresses, and the SS officers used their regained energy to brush their uniforms and polish their boots. They were enthusiastic when they heard one of their battle songs over the radio. They banged their fists on the table and sang so loud it could be heard through the entire boat:

> *"Wir werden weiter marschieren*
> *bis alles in Scherben fällt*
> *denn heute gehört uns Deutschland*
> *und morgen die ganze Welt."*

"We'll continue marching
'til everything is gone.
Today we own Germany,
Tomorrow the entire world."

"Turn it off!" Brinker called to the radio operator. He was angry because he had heard this song of the marching Hitler Youth for years. He remembered the first verse:

> *"Es zittern die morschen Knochen*
> *der Welt vor dem großen Krieg... "*

"The world's rotten bones are trembling
in fear of the coming war... "

That was how the Nazis whipped up the teens for war.

"Don't these idiots know that more than half of Germany is overrun by the Allies?" he asked the first watch officer. "Do they still believe in conquering the world?"

The chief engineer turned to Brinker. "Did you hear what the sailors in the bow room did to Krantz when he recovered from nausea?" the chief engineer asked Brinker.

"*Nein*, what happened?"

"They arranged a mock ceremony and promoted him to SS *Fischfuttermeister* - Fish Feeding Master, with the privilege to wear a net shirt as uniform. They gave him a shirt and toasted him with mineral water."

"And how did he take it?"

"He was mad as hell, but he tried not to show it. I'm sure if we'd been on shore, he'd have killed them all."

"That's all right. I'm glad the boys haven't lost their sense of humor. They're going to need it."

The skipper sat down with the chief engineer, Lieutenant Topper, and the first watch officer, Helms. Topper asked, "Every day more cities in Germany are taken by the Allies. What are we still doing here in this miserable place?"

"We're obeying orders like donkeys," Helms replied.

"We're too well-trained," Brinker admitted. "A donkey would've resisted the Nazis."

"I agree," Helms said. "Now they have infiltrated even our boat."

"Soon they'll try to give us orders," Topper said.

"Bauer has sent us on an unusual mission," the skipper said. "First we were ordered to attack Murmansk convoys. Instead we're now heading for southern Greenland."

Topper grinned. "To raise the Nazi flag over there?"

Helms laughed. "No. Over New York!"

His laughter stopped as piercing bells rang. "*Alarm! Tauchen!* — Dive!*" sounded over the intercom. They recognized the second watch officer's tense voice.

Everyone ran to their diving stations. Brinker and the chief engineer hurried to the control room. Diesels stopped, electromotors started. Hydroplanes turned. The boat dove on an incline of 20 degrees. Whoever didn't have an immediate task clung onto anything firm. Mugs, plates, books slid from the tables, fell pounding over the deck until they hit the forward bulkhead. Loud hissing and gargling noises from water gushing into the diving tanks filled the air.

"What happened?" Brinker asked Lt. Schroeder, the second watch officer, who stood in the command center.

"Two airplanes at starboard turned toward us."

Brinker quietly ordered, "To 100 meters!"

"To 100 meters," repeated Helms standing behind two sailors

at the hydroplanes.

The sudden quiet was nerve-racking. Everyone stared at the skipper. Brinker thought, we survived twenty-two attacks by airplanes. What'll happen this time?

Pitch, pitch, pitch, pitch. Depth charges crashed into the water above them. Everyone heard the devilish sound. Tension in the air was as tight as a piano string. Brinker guessed the four were pretty near.

Five seconds may be all that's left! Brinker's brain immediately ran at highest speed. Childhood. Navy training. U-boat commander. Marriage. Knight's Cross. Now? Over? Death?

Pong, pong, pong, pong. Depth charges exploded! The boat quivered. Brinker stood in the combat center, clinging to a pipe. His legs slid to the side, his ears hurt. His hands locked desperately around a pipe to hold his body from falling. His head banged against a valve handle. Two men crashed to the floor, yelling in pain. A crash of glass — all light bulbs broke.

Complete darkness.

Silence. Time seemed to stay still.

A flashlight blinked.

God, we're still alive! Brinker thought. We survived this one. I just watched my entire life pass by.

How close had the depth charges been?

He grabbed the intercom. "Any leaks in the boat?" At least the intercom works.

More flashlights lit up. Machinists replaced broken bulbs. Brinker saw the eyes of his men staring at him.

"Reaching eighty meters," Helms's voice cut through the anxiety-filled air. His words broke the tension.

Krantz and Steltner appeared at the combat center, their faces pale like chalk. "What happened?" Krantz asked, his voice unsteady.

"Stay at your diving station!" the commander ordered. "Airplanes overhead. Back to the torpedo room!"

Both disappeared at once.

"Reaching one hundred," Helms reported calmly.

Ch, ch, ch, ch.

Oh God, more are coming! Brinker thought.

Pang, pang, pang, pang after only two seconds. Depth charges detonated with ear-splitting noise. The boat shuddered. The DCs seemed to be farther away, even higher up, but still a murderous roar of four blasts against the hull shook the boat back and forth.

"Boat at one hundred meters," Helms said.

"Keep it there!" Brinker ordered.

Silence.

The bow section was rising.

A voice from the rear section. "Flood damage in engine room."

"Chief engineer to diesels!" Brinker ordered. Crew members moved aside to let the engineer through. Brinker felt the stern sinking and the bow coming up. Either too much water flowing into the engine room or the movement of the SS men had disturbed the trim of the boat.

Dammit, I told them to stay at their diving station! Where is their discipline?

"Water from rear ballast to bow!" Brinker called. Ballast pumps began to whirr. But the bow still rose. Everyone had to hold on to something, The incline rose steadily, became dangerous.

Brinker yelled into his mike: "*Alle Mann voraus, marsch, marsch!* - All men forward, rush, rush!"

Everyone who could leave his diving station ran or crawled forward. The boat was in an awkward situation that didn't change. After a minute that seemed like an hour, Brinker felt the boat swinging back into horizontal position. "All men back to diving stations!" he ordered.

The crew dashed back to their stations and the chief engineer returned to the combat center. "Water leaked from a broken cooling water valve," he reported. "Secondary valve took over. We're pumping bilge out."

"*Danke*," Brinker nodded, relieved. But what would happen if there were more depth charges? "To one hundred fifty meters!"

he ordered. There wasn't much he could do to escape the depth charges. The boat was defenseless under water against such an attack. As the boat went deeper, calm set in, now and then interrupted by dins like huge sledge hammer blows against the hull.

"Boat at 150 meters," Helms reported.

Brinker thought about the enormous water pressure on the hull and its welded seams. He turned to the boatswain. "Hartmann, did we have the same welders in the shipyard?"

"Yes, sir. I asked the *Baumeister* for the same workers we always had."

"At this water depth one bad welding seam and we're gone," said the chief engineer.

Brinker asked Schroeder, "What aircraft did you see?"

"Couldn't make them out, sir," the young lieutenant replied. "Counted two coming at us through the low clouds."

"Good job, Schroeder," the skipper said. "Could've turned out bad for us."

Silence.

Everyone waited.

The silence became unbearable.

"*Auftauchen*! - Surface! I want to get out!" a young machinist yelled with all his force. "I hate the war! Do you hear? I want out! Surface! Now!" he screamed, pounding his fists against the bulkhead.

Boatswain Hartmann reached for the claustrophobic machinist, his arms holding the young man in a tight grip. "Be quiet! It'll be over in a few minutes!" Other crew members near the two men whispered reassurances. Hartmann stroked the sweaty forehead of the trembling machinist, whose pants were wet and smelled awful. "It's over pretty soon. Only a few more minutes."

Meanwhile, the chief engineer used every trick he knew to trim the boat and make it as neutrally buoyant as possible. Finished, he moved his head at the skipper. Brinker nodded back in a nonverbal acknowledgement of the silent report.

"How long can those bastards stay above us?" Helms asked Brinker.

"Even Sunderlands can't stay longer than an hour. They have a long trip back to base from here. We'll stay down for another hour," the skipper said, "then surface and go west toward Greenland. Maybe this way we can avoid destroyers. They'll surely send them after us."

How many hours before reaching Greenland? Brinker wondered. A sudden thought made him wince. It would probably depend on how many icebergs they had to avoid.

12. Bath, England - April 8, 1945.

A young British lieutenant met Erik Svensen at the military airport near Bath. "How was the flight?" the lieutenant asked as they stepped into the British jeep.

"Too cloudy. It's a miracle the pilot found the airport."

Moving through Bath at dawn, Erik understood why this small town, 180 miles west of London, was known as one of the most beautiful cities in England. Passing the "Crescents" — large elegant housing complexes built of yellowish sandstone in a semi-circle — they finally arrived at an old three-story house. The OSS office, Naval Intelligence, the Maritime Unit of the British Secret Intelligence Service and MI-5, occupied the same building. Erik went into his office to pull some maps and sketches relevant to Hardanger Fjord from his file cabinet. Then he went to the conference hall.

A large, bare table and eight chairs stood in the middle of the otherwise empty room. The walls were covered with nautical charts, sketches of fjords and city maps. Four red ash trays sat on the table.

OSS Colonel Robert Jones, a trim, man with a stolid face, entered the meeting room, his pipe in one hand. He tapped Erik's shoulder: "Welcome back!"

Erik turned and shook the colonel's hand. "Glad to be back."

"I should think so. Want to hear more about this U-boat of yours."

Three OSS officers entered the room and greeted Erik cordially, kidding him about his dirty, smelly fisherman's clothes and blond bristles on his unwashed face.

Jones called the group to order and went to the wall chart of the Hardanger Fjord. "Well, what have you observed?"

Erik reported the events of his two days above the fjord in detail. He often consulted his notebook for times and data.

The four officers listened attentively. When Erik mentioned the submarine and its cylinders, Jones signaled to one of the officers, who left and soon returned with sketches and photographs of German U-boats.

"Show us the type you saw," Jones said when Erik finished his report. Jones pointed to a photo of a plump boat with a wide deck. "Was it like this one?"

Erik hesitated. "I'm not sure. No, it looked like this one." He held up a picture.

"Were there tanks at the side like these?" Jones asked, pointing to another photo.

"No. The lines were simple and straight like this."

"Then it's a type IX boat," Jones said. He kept the picture and pushed the others away. "The containers they removed from the sub were torpedo storage containers. Boats keep them above the pressure hull under deck. Strange, very strange to replace them with others. And SS men. Peculiar. The SS has never had any contact with the *Kriegsmarine*. Why now?" He looked at his watch, then turned to his officers. "Admiral McIntire is expecting us. MI-5 wants to be informed."

Colonel Jones and Erik went to the MI-5 admiral's office. Admiral John McIntire, Royal navy, was a heavy-set, jovial man in his sixties. He shook hands with Erik and greeted Jones before seating himself at a small desk.

Erik gave his report a second time. The sparsely furnished room filled with smoke as the admiral puffed away on a well-worn pipe. The mention of the SS officers brought the admiral forward in his chair, his eyes aglow with excitement. "That's Himmler and his cronies!" he said, knocking his pipe against an oversized ash tray. "He's through with Hitler and company. He wants to escape to Argentina." Scraping out the pipe bowl, his face was alive with determination. "We must catch those blokes. Alive! Wouldn't that be something — taking Himmler to court!" The admiral tamped new tobacco into his pipe and called his aide, ordering him to bring the latest Himmler reports from the files. Then he lit the tobacco.

Jones tried to bring the admiral back to the events at the Hardanger Fjord. "We believe the Germans have developed a new, high-explosive bomb," he said. "Because of a possible danger to the population they shifted its development from Germany to Norway."

The return of the admiral's aide interrupted Jones. The young officer handed two sheets of paper to the admiral. McIntire scanned them and smiled triumphantly. With a red pencil he underlined several lines, then passed the messages to Jones.

Jones read aloud: "On March 30, SS *Reichsführer* Himmler and his staff flew from Berlin to the south, probably to Obersalzberg. Believed they discussed reorganizing defence of the Alps." From the second sheet: "Himmler took a plane to Oslo for an unknown reason. April first."

Triumph radiated from the admiral's eyes. "See? Himmler wants to save his own life by escaping on a U-boat. I think he took gold, jewelry and paintings to the factory to stow in those cylinders. How do we catch him? Think, gentlemen!" He laid his pipe on the ash tray and picked up the telephone, dismissing the visitors with a wave of his hand.

Erik, somewhat bewildered, retired with Colonel Jones. Was McIntire crazy? Or could he be right? Was Himmler one of the six SS men on board the U-boat? But Erik admitted to himself that he had never thought of that possibility.

"Admiral McIntire was taken out of retirement like a lot of others," Jones said in the hallway outside the admiral's office. "But he's a cagy old sailor."

Erik fought off exhaustion, yawning widely.

In the cafeteria Erik could hardly keep his fork in his hand. His yawns were now coming non-stop.

"You need a nap and a bath," Jones said.

Erik nodded. He didn't need a nap, he needed a long, deep sleep.

In the office, an orderly said: "Sir, this just came in."

Erik read:

"04/09/45: Copy 5 of 5 - RAF 567/88/6310
TWO RECONNAISSANCE PLANES WING 43 ATTACKED U BOAT 60 MILES NORTH OF

ICELAND. DROPPED 8 DEPTH CHARGES AT
16:33 AND 16:49. U BOAT DESTROYED.
SGT. MURPHY - LT. BROMFIELD.
END. 55/394 PC-RW KEFLA. ICELD."

Erik read the message through twice, his weary brain having
trouble with the words.

Jones said, "If that's your submarine, it's at the bottom of the
ocean. And with it Himmler and his treasures."

Erik read the message once more before he replaced it on the
desk. "How can we be sure the sub was sunk?"

"These messages are usually correct," Jones said.

Erik wasn't satisfied. Did the pilots see air bubbles or oil
leaks? "I want to speak with the two pilots."

Jones leaned back. "Erik, you're tired. Go to bed. I'll try to
find out more details." He ordered a jeep and sent Erik off to the
Queen Victoria Hotel.

Seventeen hours later. Erik showered, shaved and ordered
breakfast to his room. He then dressed and went back to Jones'
office.

The colonel was furious. "Imbeciles!" he shouted. "Do you
know what happened? The pilots who found the sub reported
only they dropped eight depth charges. The wing commander
took it upon himself to modify the message by adding the words:
U BOAT DESTROYED."

Erik shook his head.

Jones said, "I spoke to the pilots myself. Sergeant Murphy
dropped four depth charges but can't confirm that they hit the
submerged sub. The other plane attacked later although the
location of the target was doubtful. So we keep after it. Let's
give the project a name."

"Fire Alarm," said Erik.

"Why Fire Alarm?"

"I remember MILORG men read *PROJEKT FEUER ALARM*
on boxes transported to Hardanger Fjord."

"Are you sure?"

"Per Ulfung told me. I've been thinking about it since I woke up. I don't believe the Himmler story."

"But Erik, think about the extreme security you saw."

"That simply tells us a new weapon is involved."

Jones said, "Would Himmler send so many SS men to guard a factory? So many ships to protect the loading of a weapon? When the war is almost over? No, Erik. I believe the admiral is right. These security measures were organized by Himmler to protect his own boarding of the submarine."

"But Olaf saw trucks driving every day into the factory," exclaimed Erik." I saw personnel in white laboratory coats around the factory. They brought out the empty wooden crates and burned them away from the factory. There were always half a dozen ambulances nearby. Whatever they were handling is terribly dangerous."

Jones laughed and shook his head. "You could imagine that even Hitler was on board that U-boat! What you saw was nothing other than a big cover-up!"

"I disagree. Nazi leaders would prefer to kill themselves than to flee in a U-boat."

Jones sighed and got up. "Let's report to the admiral."

Admiral McIntire, informed by Colonel Jones of the message of sinking a U-boat and its later correction, repeated his assumption that Himmler was on the submarine, and ordered another thorough search for the U-boat with planes and destroyers. He'd prefer to seize it intact, along with Himmler and the treasure. Turning to Erik, he said, "Good job, Major. I want you to stay on this project. We have to find that U-boat if it still exists!"

13. Near Quadrant AK 5587 - April 9, 1945.

U-888 cruised parallel to the coast of Greenland at a distance of 60 nautical miles. The men on the bridge enjoyed the mild wind from the west and the great visibility. Even though the sun had set an hour ago, clouds could be seen on the northern horizon almost a hundred miles away.

"Look! At 180 degrees," shouted one of the two sailors on watch. "Looks like big guns are firing?"

"Right. The clouds light up," Schroeder, the second watch officer, confirmed. "Pretty far away."

"Who are they shooting at?" Hartmann asked.

The watch officer called into the boat: "Skipper to the tower!"

"There again!"

"I can't see any ship," the sailor complained. "And I can't hear anything."

"*Dummkopf*! They're past the horizon," Hartmann burst out.

"Again, but the light stays on."

"That's an aurora, a Northern Light," Schroeder said. "We had one in January."

Brinker appeared on the tower. "What's happening, Schroeder?"

"Sir, an aurora borealis. Right astern. We thought at first there were flashes from big guns firing."

"There again. Now higher up. And it stays," Hartmann added.

"Great sight," Brinker said. "You'll see it for some hours."

"At first it was yellowish and red. Now it's bluish. See how it wavers and flickers."

"Don't forget the look-out!" the skipper said. Then he went below again.

After a while one sailor said, "Last time we saw a Northern Light we got three destroyers on our neck. Barely made it home. Auroras bring bad luck."

As soon as the boat arrived in quadrant AK 5587, Brinker ordered Helms to bring Krantz to the wardroom. "Tell him the quadrant has been reached."

Krantz arrived with an envelope. He opened it and took out two sets of documents, one set for Brinker and one for himself.

Helms picked up the now empty envelope and read:

"*OPERATION FEUER ALARM* — Order No.3"

Krantz glared at the first watch officer, said nothing, but cracked his knuckles.

"To Cuba?" Brinker said aloud, shaking his head. "Who planned this? We don't have enough fuel for such a long patrol. We probably can't even make it one way. And how could we return?"

Krantz sat even more stiffly in his chair. "The superior SS staff worked on these orders and planned the patrol. The *Kriegsmarine* will be blamed for any mistakes."

Angrily, Brinker underlined a few words and handed the first page to Helms, who silently read the underlined words:

"... drive to the next travel goal: Cuba...."

"Who the hell wrote this order?" Brinker asked. "A submarine doesn't drive and it doesn't have any travel goals. Dammit! We have quadrants of action. We aren't a travel group! This is a U-boat!"

Krantz bent forward, then jerked up again. "These are unimportant details. However, our mission must be carried out. Every order has to be executed precisely."

Brinker kept reading and marked a section with a pencil, then threw it over to Helms who read:

"...The U-boat commander may choose the most favorable course to reach the Northwest coast of Cuba where the containers will be activated. Any contact with hostile ships or planes must be strictly avoided. Activation of containers is directed exclusively by SS *Standartenführer* Krantz who will be assisted by five SS officers.

The mission of this patrol is to activate the new weapon the *Führer* has built to achieve the final victory over the evil powers of World Communism and

Plutocracy."

Helms was stunned. The containers they had loaded would make Germany win the war? And of all places from Cuba? Was everyone in Berlin crazy?

Brinker shook his head. "I can't believe this comes from the *BdU*," he said, tapping the paper with his finger.

"As I already said, this march order has been worked out by the superior SS staff and signed by the *BdU*," Krantz remarked stiffly. "It's an honor for you to be selected to put the miracle weapon into action which our revered *Führer* decided to release now. It'll change the outcome of the war and lead to the final victory, so intensely expected by millions of German men and women."

Brinker pointed to the signatures. "I read *Standartenführer* Schmeltzer and an almost illegible Martin Bonnan. Who are these people? Who is Bonnan?"

Krantz's face twisted with fury. "Bormann! Martin Bormann," he yelled, banging his fist on the table. "Don't you know the confidant of the *Führer*?"

Brinker stroked his growing blond beard. "Never heard of him. We're sailors, we aren't involved in politics."

"Politics? Our party is our nation!" Krantz barked. "Hitler, Himmler, Bormann are the personification of Germany and our party. They have created our Thousand-Year-Reich."

"We aren't party members," the skipper said. "We're officers and soldiers of the *Kriegsmarine*. There's a difference."

"That will all be changed after our victory! The SS will then take over the armed forces of our nation." His hands shook with agitation. He continued, "After reaching Cuba we'll use the secret weapon. Shoot our rockets toward America."

Brinker and Helms looked up in surprise. Topper awoke and moved his bunk curtains aside and stared at Krantz.

The skipper asked: "You're going to shoot rockets? Where are they? In the containers?"

"You guessed right," Krantz said with an expression of pride on his face. "The Miracle Weapon has been secretly developed by German scientists after years of tremendous effort. It is so dangerous it wasn't assembled in Germany but in Norway." An arrogant smile distorted his lips. "Only leading SS doctors and officers know the facts. Soon the whole world will see what we have accomplished. Those devils, Churchill and Stalin, will surrender as soon as the American continent is infested. Roosevelt and millions of Americans will die."

"Man," Brinker said. "Do you understand what you're saying?"

"I don't expect mere sailors to understand what it means," the SS colonel said. "All you have to do is see to it that we reach Cuba. Understand?"

"I have a fuel problem," Brinker said.

"That's *your* job. I can't help you." Krantz stood up, took his set of documents and left for the torpedo room.

Brinker said to his first watch officer: "Let's go up. I need some fresh air." Both men climbed to the conning tower and went to the farthest ack-ack gun platform.

"They're insane," Brinker said in a low voice. "They're all insane."

"Exactly," Helms agreed. "What can we do? What did he mean about infesting the American continent?"

"I know only that Krantz is a lunatic! We have to find out more about his plans."

"Do you think he is on a suicide mission?"

"If so, I'll make damn sure he doesn't take us with him. I'm not risking my boat and crew until I know what these guys intend to do."

"Could we make it to Cuba on the fuel we have?" Helms asked.

"I'll discuss the fuel situation with you, Topper and Schramm," Brinker knit his brows. "Why did the *BdU* sign such a ridiculous order? It doesn't make any sense. We can't return without refueling."

They both went back into the boat where Brinker called for his chief engineer and navigator Schramm.

In the wardroom, as Brinker was discussing a route to Cuba with Topper, Schramm, Helms and Hartmann, Krantz suddenly appeared.

Krantz stood in the passageway, his eyes studying each man in turn. Brinker told him, "We're planning the route to Cuba. Refueling is our most important problem."

"I want to repeat," Krantz countered, "that you must avoid any contact with the enemy. If the containers are damaged it would mean death for all of us. Do not sail through areas which the enemy controls."

The chief engineer looked at him in disbelief. "The enemy has had control of *all the oceans* since the war began. We're lucky that bad weather and good luck have hidden us this long. We have never had such a quiet patrol as this one."

The officers studied charts, figured distances and calculated the fuel consumption at various speeds. Krantz stood in the passage way looking at one point on the bulkhead. At last the chief engineer said: "We could make it to Cuba if we go down to seven or eight knots and stay there. But how can we return?"

"We must sail at the fastest speed," Krantz interjected, "so we can use our weapon as soon as possible."

"Why do we sail to Cuba? Can't we shoot the rockets into New York, Boston and other ports?" Helms asked.

"You never learned to obey orders exactly. Don't ask questions. Do what we are ordered. Understand?"

"We don't have enough fuel. That's the problem. We have to change the order," the skipper said.

"*Verdammt*! Nothing will be changed. The order from *Führer* headquarters will be followed word by word. Understand?! Highest speed is ordered."

"We can't go faster," Brinker said firmly. "I must radio the *BdU* to request supplies from other boats for our trip. I know there are several boats near the Azores. U-854 is even close to New York."

"It's *verboten* to use the radio!" Krantz protested, storming out of the wardroom.

Brinker, relieved by Krantz's abrupt departure, began preparing the text for a radio message.

A call sounded through the entire boat: "Skipper to the bridge! Ship in sight."

Hurriedly, Brinker put on his gray leather jacket, threw his dirty white cap on his head and rushed to the tower, followed by Helms and Hartmann. All others ran to their battle stations.

On the conning tower, the third watch officer pointed to port side. "Freighter. Distance one mile behind the rain shower. Running east."

Brinker looked into the dark space. After a while his eyes adjusted and he saw a black spot. "Looks like it's going to Scotland." He called down into the control room: "New course 260!"

The sub turned west, away from the ship.

"Hope they didn't see us," Helms said. "We don't need any destroyers."

When the ship could no longer be seen, Brinker ordered, "Turn back to 185!"

A loud debate erupted from the boat's interior, increasing to hysteric yelling. Even a shot sounded. Brinker and Helms dashed toward the combat center where they were joined by the chief engineer. *Funkmaat* Abert, the radio man, ran toward Brinker, shouting: "The SS men are destroying our radio!" Blood oozed from a tear in his brown uniform sleeve. "They shot me!"

They all ran to the radio room. Too late. Three sailors lay on the deck, the SS men standing above them, assault guns in their hands. Broken tubes, wires and coils lay on the floor in a heap. The radio was destroyed.

Krantz stood in front of his men, who pointed their guns at the *Kommandant*.

"I had to destroy it," Krantz said firmly. "As the highest-ranking officer here, I assume full responsibility and I will put down any resistance. This boat sails to Cuba and there will be *no* radio messages!"

Totally surprised and powerless against the heavily-armed SS men, Brinker was revolted by this act of violence. It was clear to him that *he* was in charge of this U-boat, not the SS officers he had to transport with their mysterious weapon. He was sure his crew would stand firmly behind him.

Brinker stepped into the bow room and ordered *Torpedomaat* Tenner: "Take your men into the rear torpedo room!"

Speaking to Krantz: "I will discuss our patrol with you alone. Send your men out of the room."

"*Nein*! They'll stay here." He turned to the short SS lieutenant. "Is your gun ready?" Then to Brinker. "What's on your mind?"

"You made us deaf and dumb. We can't operate a submarine in hostile waters without guidance from the *BdU*. You have endangered our patrol — "

"You acted against my order not to use the radio!"

"I had to. We don't have enough fuel. Don't you understand that? Our success is doubtful. I protest against any interference in my job as *Kommandant* of this U-boat."

"You don't know how to serve our *Führer*. He needs absolute obedience to his orders. The SS is the only troop he can trust. We obey each order without questioning. Only that can lead to victory. We were ordered not to use the radio."

"You don't understand naval warfare. I need communication with my superiors and other boats."

"What? Your commander-in-chief accepted and signed your march order. Didn't you see his signature? That should be enough for you. He is convinced our action will guarantee the final victory! Our Fatherland needs you, *Herr Kapitänleutnant*. Take the boat to Cuba!"

"You don't know how submarines function. How much fuel do you need *after* we reach Cuba?"

"I don't know. That's written in the next order."

"I must know it *now*."

"Don't ask. Obey the order. We will see later."

Could the *BdU* have plans for refueling us? Brinker pondered agitatedly. At the next location? But it's impossible without communication! Something was dead wrong. A suspicion arose in him. The *BdU* had never let him hang in uncertainty. Surely, the SS staff was incompetent to plan a U-boat patrol. As these questions flew through his mind, his anger rose. "I'll sail the boat to our next quadrant. It seems to me that even *you* don't know what we have to do after reaching Cuba. I make you responsible for the failure of our mission."

Brinker, waiting in vain for a reply, returned to the wardroom.

14. Berlin - April 9, 1945.

Everyday life in Berlin's chancellery had become hectic. Countless messages poured in — mostly bad and depressing. Others described successes of "brave German soldiers retreating to better defensive positions." Soviet troops already approached eastern parts of Brandenburg, the region around the capital, but the people in Berlin remained optimistic. A rumor circulated that Hitler would soon release a new weapon to wipe out all American resupply of Allied troops in Europe. American and British troops would be running out of ammunition, begging the Germans for food. They'd be surrendering by the hundreds of thousands. As predicted, the *Führer* would keep his promise of the *Endsieg*, the Final Victory.

SS *Standartenführer* Schmeltzer, the colonel who had prepared Operation *FEUER ALARM*, had a stack of secret messages on his heavy oakwood desk. He thumbed through them before passing them on to staff members responsible for analyzing and evaluating them. The result would be a daily report to Himmler. Suddenly, Schmeltzer stopped. A decoded British radio message contained the story of British planes sinking a German submarine north of Iceland. His hands trembled. Beads of sweat formed on his forehead and breathing became difficult. This could be none other than the submarine that carried the miracle weapon!

He took the operation manual of Operation *FEUER ALARM* from the safe and looked for dates and planned locations of U-888. They corresponded accurately with the site of the reported sinking. There could be no doubt.

Now, everything would be over. With U-888 gone, there was no other way to win the war. He got up. Then sat down again. His knees no longer supported him. He put his head into his hands, feeling only confusion.

He sat for five minutes unable to do anything. A knocking at his door raised him, but he didn't answer. When two SS officers entered the room, he panicked. "*Raus*! Out! Dammit!" he yelled.

The officers left promptly.

The shock subsided. He could again think clearly. He rubbed his hands for a while, then looked for a moment into his open right hand as if to see into the past. His own image rose — a young man fighting after WW I in the Ehrhard Brigade against communists. Hating the government of the Social Democrats he wanted the authority of the *Kaiser* re-established. In those years Adolf Hitler was in the news, a simple soldier like himself, who was fanatically speaking against the Versailles Treaty. This caused him to join Hitler's party. He became a storm trooper, beating up communists who disturbed party rallies. With enthusiasm he greeted Hitler's rise as chancellor and *Führer*. At the beginning of the war he hoped his dream of a Greater Germany could be realized, an Aryan Empire ruling Europe. Every method, even the most brutal, seemed justified to reach this goal. He felt that the Zionists were the main enemies of this objective. The power of their money threatened to destroy the German future. Supporting Himmler's idea of eliminating the Jewish race, he was completely dedicated to Hitler, whom he considered to be the greatest field marshal of all times. When the time of battle victories was over, he believed in the final victory, because the *Führer* promised it. He also knew about the terrific effect the miracle weapon would have, having himself planned Operation *FEUER ALARM* under the strictest secrecy and worked out all details of its deployment by a U-boat. This was the devilish goal: to shoot rockets with trillions of deadly germs over the American continent. He had proposed the use of modified *Rheinbote* rockets with bio-warfare heads. And now U-888, the submarine carrying the miracle weapon, had been sunk by British planes!

From the early 1920s on he had believed in Hitler's mission to establish a Greater Germany. Like Hitler himself, who was convinced that he had been selected to do this historical job, Schmeltzer was sure of Germany's rebirth with unlimited power.

The sub gone, this belief lay shattered. The war would be lost, his ideals smashed. Knowing he could never live in a destroyed

Germany, he would rather commit suicide than surrender to the communists and be held responsible for the death of millions of Soviets, Poles, and Jews.

He read the operation manual again. No mistake. The locations and dates were indeed identical. This would mean total surrender to the communists. They would hang him.

In the bathroom he burned the fateful message about the sunken U-boat and flushed the ashes down the toilet. Back at his office, he took out his Walter pistol and shot himself in the head.

15. Bath, England - April 9, 1945.

Erik considered Colonel Jones a tough, no-nonsense officer but with a poor understanding of the European mentality. Jones didn't see that Hitler played a terrible game, always hoping that something would save him and still let him win the war for Germany. Hitler relied on astrology and a mysterious Divine Providence.

Jones told Erik that everybody in the OSS office and in MI-5 was convinced that Himmler escaped on the submarine. Admiral McIntire had even called Winston Churchill to inform him of Himmler's presence on the submarine. Therefore, they planned to let the sub sail undisturbed to Argentina or another country where the Nazis would land and be arrested by an Allied military contingent. Erik repeated his arguments — but to no avail. He decided to go to London.

Next morning Erik entered the room of the OSS ETO director William Maddox. The man looked like an ambassador, with his tailor-made dark suit and gray tie. When Erik finished his report on the sub, the director asked, "What do you think is in those containers?"

"I have three possibilities. First, a high-powered special explosive that could be used to blow up an American port like New York. Or it could be a deadly gas. Or ... something to do with radiation? Death rays? Flash Gordon stuff?"

"Could there be some pest or plague stored in the containers?" Maddox asked.

Erik stared at him. "I didn't think of that."

"I remember the flu epidemic in the 1920s. Twenty million people died worldwide, two million in the United States alone. A similar occurrence could be catastrophic. I think you should add it to your list of possibilities."

A messenger interrupted them with the latest intelligence reports. Maddox thumbed through the reports while Erik considered the horrifying prospect of germ warfare.

"Here's something you'll want to see," Maddox said, passing the flimsy paper to Erik.

04/09/45: COPY 2 OF 8 - RNHQU. 443/67/2

COLLIER SANTA MARIA REPORTS SIGHTING OF SUBMARINE ON SURFACE AT 55˚22'12" NORTH 37˚46'32"WEST AT 1815 AND 1822 04/09/45. SUB DID NOT ATTACK. CONTINUED COURSE WEST AT 1827. END.

CAPT. ELMER HERDING. 37/129/RNATL.

Erik looked at the SS Director. "That tells us that the depth charges dropped north of Iceland missed the U-boat. It's still afloat and headed for the United States."

Maddox nodded. "You'll have to fly to Washington. I'll arrange a flight on the next plane for you. But first I want you to go to the 'Citadel.' There is a man with an incredible amount of information about U-boats and their positions, Commander Winn. He also has an unerring sense about Dönitz' plans and his staff officers. Tell him everything you know about this U-boat. It's important."

The ETO's driver took Erik and Maddox' adjutant, Lieutenant Grubb, to the 'Citadel', a bunker in London's center, not far from Downing Street, where the Operational Intelligence Center was located.

Inside, Grubb led Erik way down to Submarine Tracking. Commander Winn met him and shook his hand. They went into a small cubicle where Erik reported what he had seen at the Hardanger Fjord. Winn asked him into the tracking room where they followed the U-boat's probable path on a huge chart of the Atlantic. Hundreds of tabbed pins marked positions of vessels and U-boats.

"Interesting! This boat doesn't give any reports," Commander Winn said, slowly shaking his head. "Seems to be special." After stroking his chin, he continued: "I don't believe the Himmler story. Seems too absurd. Dönitz wouldn't use one of his U-boats for such an adventure. He was an officer of the old *Kaiserliche Marine*, too honest to support people fleeing from responsibilities."

Hearing this, Erik felt relieved. "What can *you* do to identify and follow that boat?"

"I'll talk with MI-5," Winn said. "Are you aware of a U-boat sighting by a collier captain? That might be your sub." He pointed to a small tab.

Erik nodded.

"But the report must be wrong. The course going west should be going south. Otherwise, the two vessels would have passed too close together. The U-boat must have changed course for a short time to mislead the captain. I would like to stay in contact with you while you're in the United States."

At the airport Erik boarded a green and brown B-29 bomber, joining three officers flying to Iceland.

Hours later they approached the Faeroe Islands and Erik peered through the window at the steep rocks which had been formed in the Ice Age. He could see where massive glaciers had cut deep valleys. One of his fellow passengers, a pilot, knew the short tarmac on the tiny island. "It's a horrible strip between cliffs," he shouted to Erik.

Another officer grinned. "We'll make it to the Faroes. Only good pilots land here. All the bad ones have crashed and died."

The stopover in Iceland was short, with just enough time for the three officers to leave the plane, and for the pilot to receive information on the rapidly changing weather conditions. After refueling they headed for Greenland. Through a hole in the cumulus clouds below Erik saw white-capped waves on the ocean and thought about the U-boat. The bomber, tossed in the tumultuous air, occasionally dropped ten to thirty feet, then shot up again. Between clouds Greenland's vast ice cap showed shiny, silvery lines of water flowing over the ice and a few black mountain peaks protruded from the ice cover.

"We'll be in Narssarsuaq in five minutes," the pilot hollered.

When he attempted landing, the bomber hit the ground hard and was airborne again. It bumped three times before it finally taxied down the long airstrip. A heavy wind pummeled the plane as a support crew tied it to concrete blocks on the ground. The plane still shook as the bomber crew and Erik climbed out and ran to a hangar for instructions. They clasped their hands to their caps to keep them from blowing off, while the wind whipped their pants across their legs like a cat-o'nine tails. Some thirty bombers at the side of the landing strip were grounded.

"No take-off for the next twenty-four hours," the liaison officer told the pilot. "You'll find accommodations and food in building C-7."

After receiving his room assignment and eating a hearty dinner, Erik and the pilot crossed the 6,000-foot-long tarmac.

"The Vikings settled here before they reached America," the pilot told Erik. "You can still see the ruins on the other side of the fjord." He pointed to a green area behind the blue water, where bizarre-shaped icebergs floated. "Your namesake, Eric the Red, settled there."

"What are all these buildings around the airport?" Erik asked.

"Most of them belong to a huge hospital complex."

"Transit station?"

"No, the most serious cases. They must stay here until the war is over."

"Why?"

"Most are severely crippled. Nobody is supposed to see them. The sight would dampen the public's enthusiasm for the war."

The next day, April 12, the winds ceased, and Erik was flown to Frobisher Bay, Canada, north of Hudson Bay, where a long airstrip had been built for American bombers destined for Europe. After refueling, they made the last hop to a military airport near Washington, D.C.

Dead tired, Erik climbed out of the bomber. He thought of the U-boat and wondered if it had been sighted again when he noticed the American flag in front of the terminal, flying at half-mast. "What's happened?" he asked one of the ground personnel.

"Didn't you know? President Roosevelt died."

16. Washington, D.C. - April 13, 1945.

The headquarters of the Office of Strategic Services were in downtown Washington, D.C., on E and 23rd Street. Erik went immediately to the office of Major Russ Bender and found his former boss looking as young as two years ago, slim and athletic, his expression always optimistic.

They exchanged greetings and Bender grinned. "What's this about a sub coming to bomb New York? Have you been reading too many cartoons?"

"No such luck," Erik said. "There's a U-boat carrying a top-secret payload. I wish it were a joke."

Russ checked his watch. "In ten minutes we'll see Abe Weinstein. He's now the Deputy Director of Intelligence and he's taking your story very seriously. In the meantime, how about a cup of coffee?"

Russ filled two mugs, handing one to Erik. "Nothing's changed since you left. Army officers call us a group of professors, crazies and scribblers."

"Is Red Herbert still here?"

"Of course. And he's the same as before." Russ grinned.

"You should have seen how stiff the British are. Always correct. They're more formal, more inclined to agree with their superiors. Sipping tea and smoking pipes."

"Not a good experience?"

Erik waved his hand with disgust. "We had lots of trouble with the British. They didn't want us in the field, only at our desks. MI-5 wanted to keep all the action in its own hands."

"Even though you were trained in Canada by MI-5 personnel?"

"They said we were too inexperienced. "

"And the Norwegians?"

"Great. They want the Germans out. They did everything we asked."

"We have to see the DDI."

Abe Weinstein, a short man with a bald, shiny head and

77

penetrating eyes, shook Erik's hand. He was the sort of man who could free himself from conventional thoughts and grasp new concepts. "Glad to see you back! Congratulations on the fine job in Norway. I got a message from ETO." He pointed to five men in the room. "These gentlemen are all very interested in your news — they're experts on German industry and hope to help us solve your riddle." Abe seated himself at the end of the conference table. With a wave of his hand, he invited the others to be seated.

Erik glanced around. A large window behind him opened the view of the Potomac River. Two huge pictures on the side wall featured historic battles of the Revolutionary War. Eight places were set with paper pads, pencils and colored pens.

Abe picked up the phone. "Sarah, please call the two officers from Data Bank Norway."

As soon as the two tall Norwegians joined the group, Erik began his report. When he mentioned the presence of SS men on board the U-boat, the others showed surprise.

"Unusual," Weinstein murmured.

One Norwegian with a narrow face said: "We know that the Hardanger Fjord factory is run by the SS. All operating personnel and guards are SS."

One bald expert on Germany mentioned that the SS had tried in several cases to take charge of new projects. "We know that Wernher von Braun was arrested in Peenemünde by the SS because he refused to work for them instead of for the German Army."

Erik continued his report.

Abe wanted to know if there were any clues about what was packed into the torpedo tubes of the submarine.

"I can only guess," Erik answered. "It was impossible for us to get close to the factory. Norwegians reported seeing crates and boxes shipped into the factory with labels marked POISON."

A gray-haired officer across from Erik cleared his throat. "Do we know the course of the U-boat that's carrying this stuff?"

"The last sighting was south of Greenland heading west," a

young analyst with a blond beard replied. "The target could be Boston or New York."

"British Submarine Tracking believes the real course could be south," Erik interjected.

A skinny young officer bent forward. "Did the sub give weather reports and daily location messages? Its course could be followed from that information."

"Russ, please find out about this from the navy," Abe said. "What else do we know about the U-boat?"

"I believe each container weighs a ton and a half to two tons," Erik said. "It can't be regular explosives. The impact would be negligible."

Abe nodded. "You're right. It has to be something more than regular explosives. Otherwise, the Germans would have produced it in their own country. There has to be a reason why they worked in Norway. It must present a danger if not handled properly."

"What are you thinking, Abe?" Russ asked.

"Germ warfare. It's ETO's idea and I go along with it. I want a report — as fast as you can put it together — of all possible explanations for the factory at Hardanger, germ warfare, or whatever. Give me your best guesses on the potential mission of this U-boat, and give me the latest dope on the developments coming out of Germany. Make a list of the countermeasures to be taken to intercept that sub. I want all this by 1700 tomorrow."

Silence.

"Thank you," Abe said. "See you tomorrow."

Erik and Russ were working in Russ' office when a new message arrived. Russ read it, smiled and passed it on to Erik.

04/12/45:   COPY 2 OF 3 ETO LONDON 65/7/1 URGENT FOR DDI AND 331: CANADIAN RECON PLANE REPORTS SIGHTING OF SUB AT 0808 04/12 WITH COURSE SWS 400 N.MILES EAST OF ST.JOHNS NEWFDLD. AS ORDERED PLANE DID NOT ATTACK, BUT KEPT DISTANCE.

W.MADDOX. END. 66/289 OSS ETO LDN.

Erik threw the paper on the desk. "A German sub prowling off the coast and we don't dare sink it! It makes my blood boil. That's the result of McIntire's decision."

Later that day, the task force of experts assembled in Bender's large office to work on possible missions against the sub. They discussed reports from Germany on the latest inventions and projects. The Norwegian officers dwelt on the nature of the crates marked POISON shipped from Oslo to Hardanger Fjord. They checked messages about heavy water production and atomic research. Notes about the two physics professors Hahn and Heisenberg were reviewed but didn't show anything suspicious. The German atomic research, based on the use of heavy water, had been stopped by the raid on Ryukan. Erik heard for the first time that there had been tests with rockets launched from a U-boat underwater in the Baltic Sea. *Kapitänleutnant* Steinhoff, Helmut Weiss and Wernher von Braun, had developed the concept. A photo went from hand to hand, showing a missile emerging from the sea and taking off like a comet. Someone had written on the backside:

U-511, Baltic Sea, June 4, 1942.

Erik interjected: "I believe these guys are changing naval warfare for the future."

"They've already changed the weapons for the next war," Russ said.

Project *TEST STAND 12* was briefly discussed. It involved launching V-2 missiles against New York from containers towed by U-boats to the U.S. coast. Could the submarine be carrying smaller missiles, produced in the Hardanger Fjord factory? The *Rheintochter* and the smaller *Rheinbote* missiles could be used on a submarine. The latter had shot small warheads against Antwerp.

"Could the containers be used as missile launchers?" Russ asked.

"Absolutely possible," Erik answered. "The rods at one end of the containers could be used to erect them."

Two officers discussed data on medical research on epidemics and contagious diseases. "The Nazis did lots of tests in concentration camps with inmates," one analyst said. "We should look into these reports. I remember tests with 'yellow fever' in Buchenwald, malaria in Ravensbrück, and sterilization tests reported by two Poles escaping from Buchenwald."

"But these aren't relevant. They can't be easily disseminated and they're working slow," Dr. Rosensaft said. "The Germans had a vaccination against it. They must have other things in mind."

"How's botulism?" Erik asked.

"Oh, *clostridium botulinum* can be cultured in large amounts," said Rosensaft, expert on bio-terrorism. "And if distributed into the water supply of cities, they can cause tremendous effects. This stuff is the most poisonous substance we can think of. The bacteria produce this toxin and it can wipe out whole populations."

"Has this ever been planned by someone?"

"The Germans once thought of spraying a cloud of this stuff over the west coast of England, hoping the winds would spread the cloud, killing the British, but dissolve before reaching Germany."

"Didn't the Belgians work in this field before the war? The Nazis must have found their information."

"The Krauts dropped the tests, fearing the cloud would still be strong enough when it reached Germany to kill Germans."

"But they wouldn't be afraid to use it on America?"

"Of course not."

"How about 'yellow cross,' 'white cross' and nerve gases?"

"Hitler was afraid these gases would do more harm to the Germans than to other nations," Dr. Rosensaft said. "He'd personally experienced the effects of gas, being blind during 1917. I don't believe the Nazis would use them. But they could use *pasturella pestis*, causing an epidemic of the plague. In nature fleas carry the bacteria. The Nazis could spread them after aerolizing them."

"Terrible," Erik said. "The black death repeated in this century on our continent!"

"We'd have to isolate the infected. There's no vaccine to fight this disease."

"What's the plague like?"

"Typically, plague follows a bubonic course. It's acute two to seven days after exposure. Fever, headache, shaking chills, pain in the groin or neck, nausea, vomiting and diarrhea. Swelling may become excruciatingly painful. If plague pneumonia is added, damage would be dangerous. Most cases are fatal." The doctor made a short pause. "But there are many organisms the Germans could use. I'll show you what known stuff could be a threat to us." He went to the blackboard and wrote a list of possible bio materials:

TYPE:	AGENT:	DEATH RATE:	
		Untreated:	Treated:
typhoid	*salmonella typhosa*	4-20	2-5
cholera	*vibrio comma*	10-60	5-30
meliodosis	*pseutomonas pseudomallei*	95-100	50-?
anthrax	*bacillus anthracis*	95-100	5-20
plague	*pasteurella pestis*	30-60	0-5
tularaemia	*francisella tularensis*	0-60	0-10
brucellosis	*brucella*	2-20	2-5
influenza		0-10	0-3

"The columns for the death rate show how many of every 100 persons, untreated and treated, would die," Dr. Rosensaft explained. "Only those bacteria with high death rate would be used."

"Horrible! What men can think of," Abe said.

"These numbers sound catastrophic," the doctor continued, "but you must bring enormous numbers of organisms to the region in order to have a devastating effect on the population. Churchill wanted to employ bio-warfare against the Nazis, if they would use it against the British. In 1942 he ordered a study.

English scientists came up with anthrax, being disseminated by air-bursting bombs. They estimated that more than 40,000 bombs were required to kill half the inhabitants of six large German cities."

"I am suspicious the Germans have worked on bacteria or viruses much more horrible than what you're thinking of," the Norwegian said. "Otherwise they would have done the job in their own country. It must be very dangerous. I believe the Germans are capable of producing such murderous weapons."

"I believe so too," Rosensaft said. "The U-boat cannot carry that many organisms of those I listed to do considerable damage to our population. I'm expecting the most horrible bacteria from them. They have accomplished so many new weapons and developments. Fortunately, Hitler and his uneducated cronies directly around him make one mistake after another."

"How can these bacteria be disseminated?" Erik asked.

"They would be dispersed in a form of aerosol," Rosensaft explained. "The projectile might have a small cylinder of compressed air to direct an air current up through the powdered agent and out of an exit port."

"How long can these bacteria be kept alive?"

"They have a limited life when stored. Their biological activity is declining over time. But who knows what the Nazis have developed? Important also is the climate, I mean temperature, humidity and so on, to activate the organisms when dispersed."

"The human species is the most horrible animal," said the tall Norwegian. "Don't forget, Hitler's talking about the 'Miracle Weapon' that'll give him the final victory. This propaganda slogan keeps the Germans fighting."

The phone rang. Russ picked it up and listened. He hung up and said, "The Navy reports that our sub is the only U-boat in the area and it still maintains silence. The Navy intercepts calls from the region around the Azores. Lots of U-boats in that area. Many in the northern regions."

"I'm convinced I'm right," Erik said. "U-888 is trying to sneak across on a solo mission."

"The more I hear, the more I'm sure its cargo is deadly. It's scary, Major," Russ said. He looked at the team. "We have a long night ahead of us."

18. Atlantic, about 30° N - April 14, 1945.

Brinker was enraged so much by Krantz's action that he had to brace himself to stay calm and think of how to lead his crew against the SS intruders. One SS man had shot radio operator Abert, fortunately causing only a slight arm wound that had almost healed. Three more shots had been fired into the radio room. The shooting could have damaged the boat itself. Krantz's higher rank gave him no authority to issue orders without Brinker's approval. Assault guns had never been used on any submarine. The SS officers had obviously smuggled them aboard in their kit bags. Brinker wanted to kill the SS men but the pistol in his safe was the only small weapon allowed him on the boat. Strong discipline also held Brinker back. Two SS men sat continuously in the bow room, guns in their hands. There were more weapons for the rest of them. Never had outsiders been on a submarine with hand weapons! To remind the crew that they were different, the SS men shaved daily, Krantz even twice.

Brinker remembered the farewell words of *Kapitän* Bauer who warned him about his uninvited guests.

Hartmann had reported to his skipper that Krantz asked the bridge watch if they suffered from nausea, headache or fever? He also wanted to know if one of the ten containers had any leaks. That, at least, was understandable. Krantz was concerned about possible leakage of the containers after the depth charge explosions near the boat. But why had Krantz destroyed the radio? Why was he against discussing the fuel problem with the *BdU*? Was it all foul play?

Brinker took the three SS orders for Operation *FEUER ALARM* from the safe and re-read them, his eyes lingering on the signatures of the *BdU*. He took an older document and compared the signatures. "Godt" looked somewhat different on the SS orders. Could someone have forged the signature of Commander-in-Chief Submarines Admiral Godt? The last signatures definitely looked different from those on older documents.

Brinker realized the SS may have deceived the staff of the *Kriegsmarine* and obtained the U-boat for this patrol by a trick! Perhaps the Commander-in-Chief U-boats didn't even know the boat's actual mission. Wasn't there only an original of the SS order? Strange. And no copy for the flotilla, not even for the *BdU*! This had never happened. Why had they received a new number, U-888? Was this a fakery, too? Comparing the signatures again he now saw that Admiral Godt's was definitely false!

Should he turn around and take the boat back to Wilhelmshaven or Trondheim, risking his own arrest and the possibility of a court-martial? Would Dönitz protect him against the Nazis? Until now, the admiral had kept the influence of the *Partei* away from the *Kriegsmarine*.

Brinker thought about the situation in Germany, where large regions were already occupied by enemy forces. The last reports they'd heard over the radio had been terrifying. In the west, the cities of Trier, Cologne and Mainz were overrun by the Americans; in the east, Danzig and Königsberg had been taken by the Soviets. In the south, Baden, Kassel and Würzburg had fallen into the hands of the Americans. How long until all of Germany was occupied? Before they reached Cuba the war could be over, the German navy surrendered to the British. And how could they be refueled even if the next order would give him precise rendezvous conditions for meeting the supply vessel? Hadn't the time schedule for reaching Cuba at all been completely ruined by the slow speed the boat was making? And if they could not be refueled, it was senseless to even think of returning to Germany!

Krantz's words came to mind: "Churchill and Stalin will surrender when the American continent is infested, and Roosevelt and millions of Americans die." Would U-888 and its crew die too?

Brinker sought out Helms and Hartmann on the conning tower and stepped over to the farthest ack-ack gun platform with them.

He said under his breath, "Listen! I found the SS falsified Godt's signature on the operation orders. They stole our boat from the *BdU*."

"My God!" Helms whispered, eyes wide. "Does the *BdU* even know where we are?"

"No. We're in this alone. The war will be over soon. It's insane to fire rockets at America. I refuse to let them use this boat to kill millions of people."

"How will you stop them?"

"Bosun, learn more about Krantz's plans to launch the weapon."

Hartmann nodded.

"We'll go to Cuba," Brinker continued. "Render the miracle weapon useless and surrender when the war is over. It's safer to sail to Cuba than to go back through the North Atlantic, with all the American aircraft carriers, planes, destroyers and corvettes. Too many boats have been lost in the last weeks. We've been lucky, had unusually few enemy contacts on this patrol."

"*Jawoll, Herr Kaleu.*" Helms said. "What if we kill the SS men? We can pick them off one at a time."

"It's better first to find a way to discover Krantz's complete plans. Don't talk about what I told you!"

"*Jawoll, Herr Kaleu.*"

The skipper, feeling more relaxed now that he had a course of action, called the chief engineer, the first watch officer and the navigator to the wardroom to discuss the safest cruise to the quadrant near Cuba specified in the operation order.

The navigator studied the charts. "Do you intend to go north or south of Cuba to our next point of action?" he asked.

"The course off-shore of Florida seems too dangerous," the chief engineer said. "Besides, we'd have to run against the Gulf Stream which would cost us additional fuel."

"The Bahama Islands will force us to cruise very close to the Florida coast," Schramm said. "It's better to go through the Caribbean Sea."

"Our boats haven't been there for some time," Brinker said. "I don't think we'll encounter many destroyers in that region."

The navigator and chief engineer agreed that their former estimate of eight knots was still the highest and most economical speed.

Brinker dismissed them, then told Helms, "Bring Krantz to the wardroom. I want you to stay with us while we talk. I want you informed on everything we do."

When Krantz and Helms entered, Brinker invited them to sit down. Krantz sat stiffly.

Brinker pointed to the chart, his finger on the entrance to the Caribbean Sea west of Puerto Rico. "We'll sail south until we go through Mona Passage into the Caribbean Sea toward Cuba. It is less dangerous than going against the Gulf Stream."

"Is that really the safest way?" Krantz interrupted. "We should avoid every possible contact with the enemy."

Brinker raised an eyebrow. "This *is* the safest way. We'll pass the Guantánamo Bay naval base at a safe distance south of Cuba." He pointed to the place on the chart.

Seeing Krantz staring at the chart, Brinker said: "The Americans at one time had many seaplanes, destroyers and subchasers at Guantánamo Bay. But now I assume they've removed them to more sensitive areas farther north."

"When will we reach our action quadrant?" demanded Krantz. "Are we sailing at maximum speed?"

"We're sailing at eight knots...."

"*Verdammte Scheisse!*" Krantz interrupted. "The march order says specifically that the highest speed should be used. 18 knots, not eight. You have to obey the order!"

"We'll sail at eight knots. Otherwise we won't reach our destination at all. Can't you understand that? We don't have the fuel to run faster. I wasn't given the complete operation order before leaving Wilhelmshaven," Brinker said coolly. "I had to read it in three phases. And I don't even know the fourth one...."

"That's the way all orders are given," Krantz said.

"Maybe that's the way an SS sergeant gets his orders for a

platoon in the field. But that method doesn't work in the *Kriegsmarine*. The commander of a vessel has to have the full information before leaving port. Had I known Cuba was the destination, I could have requested more fuel in Wilhelmshaven before starting this trip."

Krantz's face reflected his unwillingness to admit error. "Is there no way to get fuel?"

"We could refuel from other boats if we were able to ask the *BdU* where the other boats are," Brinker said, speaking carefully. "But since you destroyed the radio we can no longer communicate with *BdU* and with other boats. As I've said, the only way to reach Cuba at all is by sailing at eight knots. There is no alternative. How we are going to sail back home is another matter."

Krantz said nothing. After a minute he got up. "I have no more questions," he said, leaving Brinker and his officers in the wardroom.

"That's what he gets for destroying the radio," Brinker said more to himself than to anyone else. He went to the conning tower with Helms. "From now on, the watch on the conning tower will be kept only by officers and petty officers."

The skipper, Helms and Hartmann stepped over to the gun platform, the only location on the U-boat where he could speak without being heard. "Is there any way we can find out what Krantz's next step is?" Brinker asked. "We must know what his plans are."

"Yes, sir. I have an idea," Hartmann said. "I think I can listen unobserved to their conversation in the bow room through the voice tube near my bunk that leads from the *Torpedomaat*'s stand to the combat center."

"Good. That could be invaluable." He called to the watch officer at the front end of the tower: "*Funkmaat* Abert to the tower!"

A minute later, the radio operator saluted his skipper.

"Abert, how's your arm?"

"*Sehr gut*. Doesn't even hurt anymore."

"I need an emergency receiver and a transmitter. Can you build them with the remaining radio parts?"

"I'll try, sir," Abert said. "I've already separated all usable parts and stored them by categories."

Brinker nodded. "Don't let the SS men see what you're doing. I need this receiver. I trust you to get it done in a few days."

Helms brought up another problem. By this time on a regular patrol they would have shot several torpedoes and reloaded the tubes with the extra eels stored between the bunks below the tables. "*Herr Kaleu*, shouldn't we get rid of the two extra torpedoes in the bow room? We aren't allowed to attack enemy targets."

"That's true," the skipper said. "We'll do that right away. Get Tenner and Krantz to the wardroom."

Krantz agreed immediately. Soon they would be able to sit around the table with their legs under it. *Torpedomaat* Tenner prepared the two eels in the tubes to be shot. After ten minutes of checking them out, he reported, "Tubes one and two ready."

The skipper ordered: "Tube one, fire!"

This time, he didn't have to aim at a ship, the torpedo was simply shot to run straight through the water until its power was used up and it sank to the ocean floor. The soundman sat at his listening device and reported: "Torpedo still running." Minutes later he said: "Torpedo stopped." And briefly thereafter, "Torpedo imploded and sinking."

The skipper ordered: "Tube two, fire!"

With a hissing noise the second torpedo was sent out. The chief engineer gave orders to compensate for the lost weight of the two torpedoes. The ballast pumps hummed.

Suddenly the soundman reported: "Torpedo turning toward port side." And a minute later: "Torpedo circling. Stop the noisy pumps! I can't hear." And shortly after he yelled: "*Herr Kaleu*, torpedo running in a circle!"

"*Verdammter Dreck!*" the skipper shouted. "Still circling?"

"Yes, sir. Still circling. Turning toward us."

"Tenner! How deep is it running?" Brinker called into the

voice tube.

"*Drei meter, Herr Kaleu.*" Ten feet.

"*Scheisse!* Both diesels — full speed ahead!" The diesel engines responded. The entire boat trembled. The heavy coffee pot walked across the table in the wardroom, hit the rail and fell, splashing coffee over the deck.

"Boat's running full speed ahead," the helmsman reported from the control room.

"Where is the torpedo?" the skipper shouted to the soundman. "Port or starboard behind us?"

"Can't make it out."

Hartmann rushed to the sounding room and sat down at the listening device, putting a second set of earphones on his head. "Can't hear anything!" he yelled.

Brinker ordered: "Both diesels stop!"

The diesel engines stopped, but the propellers still made too much noise for the two men at the listening equipment. It seemed impossible to find out what the torpedo was doing behind the boat. Hartmann stared at one point on the bulkhead, then closed his eyes for better concentration.

"Dammit! What's the torpedo doing?" the *Kommandant* yelled to Hartmann, his fingers tapping the bulkhead.

After agonizing seconds, the two in the listening room looked at each other and nodded. "Torpedo behind at port side!" Hartmann shouted to the skipper.

"Both diesels full speed ahead!" Brinker responded. He looked at the gyro compass. "New course 270!" The helmsman repeated, "Course 270". Running at full speed with the rudder turned, the boat began a sharp turn to starboard. When Brinker thought they were beyond the point of collision with the circling torpedo, he shouted, "New course 200! Move rudder slowly!"

After a few minutes, the skipper ordered both diesels stopped and asked Hartmann, "Where's the eel now?"

The two men in the sounding room listened again. "Still circling, but too far away to bother us. We're safe."

Brinker felt the tension in the men around him fade. He

rejoiced. "Good that we got rid of those two devils. Reload tubes one and two! Clean up the bow torpedo room! Both diesels half-speed ahead."

U-888 resumed its slow speed, its nose pointed toward the Caribbean. Brinker felt better, knowing that the bow room was empty and ready for the action he would have to take against the SS officers.

19. Berlin - April 16, 1945.

Nervously, SS *Reichsführer* Himmler paced the floor of his sparsely furnished office in the *Führerbunker*. The plush building of the chancellery had been damaged by artillery shells in several sections and could no longer be used. He was now thirty feet below ground in a bunker with eighteen small rooms for Adolf Hitler, his top aides and a few generals. Deep pessimism was the prevailing mood among the dozen people in the bunker. Himmler was severely depressed by the latest news about the Soviet advances toward Berlin. Even Goebbels, usually joking, was short in his comments. Briefings were held less frequently. The daily review of troop movements was Hitler's only regular meeting with his remaining generals and aides.

Himmler stopped in front of a mirror and sighed deeply at the sight of his pale image. His glasses, covering his hazel eyes, made his face appear thin under the short-cut dark hair. He felt old. For two days he waited for the report from U-888. According to plan, the U-boat should have started the miracle weapon deployment on April 14. Today was April 16. Waiting for Krantz's message of success increased his uneasiness.

Suddenly he remembered NSKK *Sturmbannführer* Albrecht. Albrecht had been forced to give up a position as Hitler's naval adjutant because of a marriage scandal, but stayed as personal aide with a rank in the lowly motorized corps of the Party. Himmler knew the *Sturmbannführer* to be familiar with U-boats as a former *Korvettenkapitän*. Since Albrecht had never been briefed about the secret project, a chat with him would not reveal Himmler's fear about U-888's fate. He called Albrecht to his office.

Tall, blond and blue-eyed, Albrecht was known to all staff members to be honest and trustworthy. Because of his open character, he was well-liked by everyone in the *Bunker*.

Without pretext, Himmler opened a conversation about submarines and asked Albrecht to describe a type IX U-boat. In the middle of the presentation, Himmler interrupted Albrecht.

"How many days would it take a type IX boat from Norway to reach Cuba?"

"Between 25 and 30 days."

Irritated, Himmler asked, "Why so long?"

"U-boats can't take enough fuel to go to America and back. They have to sail more slowly than usual. ..."

"How slow?"

"Maybe eight knots."

Impatient, Himmler snarled: "How can you increase the speed of a U-boat?"

"Only by refueling from other boats at convenient locations."

Himmler bent forward. "Do we have U-boats in the Atlantic for refueling?"

"Not any more, sir. We recently lost the last boats along the American coast. And the few boats left may not even be able to return. Now our subs just make it into the North Atlantic for short-distance patrols. We're too low on oil for long trips."

"Interesting," Himmler said abruptly, barely hiding his fury. "Had Schmeltzer once talked with you about submarines?"

"No, sir. He discussed only jeeps and motorbikes with me."

"Or his successor, Kugler?"

"No, sir."

To end the meeting, Himmler said in passing, "Is Admiral Dönitz in Kiel?" He didn't even listen to the answer. But he dismissed Albrecht and picked up the telephone.

"Kugler, come over immediately!"

A moment later, *Standartenführer* Kugler entered the office. A heavy-set man in a spotless black uniform, he saluted briskly, his boots clicking. He tilted his bald head with its oversized ears backward to hide his imperfection and waited.

Himmler ignored Kugler's salute and let him stand. "How long does it take a U-boat to travel from Wilhelmshaven to Cuba?"

Kugler looked shocked. "It should be there by now. I ordered maximum speed."

"Then how do you explain why U-888 hasn't reported

deployment?"

"U-888 should have reached the location and executed its task two days ago," Kugler replied stiffly. "The plan was prepared with utmost detail. Krantz is the best man to carry out this kind of action."

Himmler was fast losing his temper. "How much fuel was on the sub?"

"Sir, there was sufficient fuel on board U-888."

Furiously, Himmler pushed his glasses up on his nose. "That's not an answer to my question. Schmeltzer and you are incompetent idiots! He's already dead," Himmler shouted. "When will *you* learn? Transmit immediately that U-888 should interrupt its radio blackout and report about its action! Contact Count Bernadotte from the Swedish Red Cross. I want to talk with him right away. I want to delay the end of the war."

"Yes, sir. Delay the end of the war," Kugler repeated. He clicked his heels, stuck his arm up in the air, and quickly left the room.

Half an hour later, an encoded message for U-888 crossed the Atlantic from Berlin. It was repeated every half hour.

Meanwhile, Kugler tried to connect with the telephone system in Sweden. He finally managed to get Count Bernadotte on the phone.

"Count, I'm conveying *Reichsführer* Himmler's wish to meet with you. Would you please tell me where and when you can meet?"

20. Washington, D.C. - April 16, 1945.

Together with Abe Weinstein, Erik entered the office of the OSS Chief General Bill Donovan at ten in the morning. They sat down at a wide conference table in the center of the room.

"These are sad times, Bill. We're going to miss FDR," Abe said.

Donovan agreed. "But our new President is a competent man. I think he's going to surprise some people."

"Of course, no question."

Donovan looked at Erik. "Is this the man who's seen the sub you're all so worried about?"

Abe introduced Erik to the director and put Bender's report on the oversize table. Still standing, he quickly summarized what Bender's team had written. The director listened attentively, his face giving nothing away.

"I'll have a meeting with the secretary," Donovan said, taking the report. "Thank you. I don't want to lose any time." An hour later he entered the War Department building.

Henry Stimson listened to Donovan's words with one ear only. "I have to see the President. Let's continue when Forrestal is present." He turned to his aide. "Call Jim. I need him with Admiral Burger." Turning back he said, "Gentlemen, I'll see you at two."

Three hours later they gathered again in Stimson's office, the door closely guarded by a security officer. Forrestal and the admiral listened intently as Donovan briefly summarized the report on the German submarine and its supposed mission.

"What do you think, Jim?" Stimson asked. "That sounds extremely dangerous. Is that sub related to the rumors about Hitler's 'Miracle Weapon'?"

"The Navy has to react," Forrestal answered. He turned to the admiral. "This sub is a terrible threat. We'd better look into it immediately."

"What are the chances that it's carrying some kind of rocket?"

Stimson asked the admiral. "The Germans have fired missiles across the Channel on England. We must be careful. This sub may be here on a suicide mission."

"We'll start the hunt immediately," Admiral Burger said.

Stimson added, "You assume there is the possibility that the containers on the sub carry some kind of lethal germ. If so, you cannot blow up the sub or damage those containers. Understood? Until we know what we're dealing with, our first priority is to hold that sub away from our shores. In the meantime, we'll keep this to ourselves. No need to alarm the public. I order top security."

Two hours later messages were sent ordering all anti-submarine forces from the Caribbean to move north. 82 vessels and 177 planes left their bases the next day. The most intensive submarine hunt of the war began.

21. Atlantic Ocean - April 19, 1945.

U-888 sailed towards the Mona Passage which leads from the Atlantic Ocean through the arching chain of islands into the Caribbean Sea. Brinker ordered the U-boat to sail on the surface to keep battery power at its maximum. The skipper, the first watch officer and *Obersteuermann* Schramm stood on the conning tower. The navigator was to guide the U-boat safely between the two islands of Santo Domingo and Puerto Rico. Under an azure sky the sun's rays warmed the men on the tower, raising their spirits. The ice-cold temperatures of the North Atlantic had been left behind. U-888 was now in a warm and humid environment. The officers were barefoot and wore only T-shirts and pants, which they had shortened by cutting off the legs above the knees. In a few hours the sub would leave the Atlantic for the last leg of its journey.

Brinker wanted to sail through the passage during dusk. Having never been in the Caribbean, he recalled colleagues' stories about American ships and planes skillfully chasing German submarines in this area. The Americans would not let U-boats attack the Panama Canal. Still, the U-boat commanders had sunk more than 1,500 ships in the Caribbean.

To Brinker's surprise nothing happened. Not a single ship was visible in the twilight. Lights on the islands were not darkened and shone peacefully. Apparently German subs were no longer feared in this region. The street lights of Mayaguez on Puerto Rico gleamed on port side as the U-boat slowly passed by the small island of Mona and slipped into the Caribbean without incident.

At this location waves from two different ocean regions meet and may run crosswise to each other. Schramm, the navigator, expected rough seas, but instead found a blue, mirror-like surface lying calmly under a golden sun in the morning watch. What a contrast to the stormy weather and foam-laden waves through which the boat had sailed only weeks ago!

Schramm stared through the pelorus at a mountain peak on the island of Santo Domingo to establish a bearing for determining the boat's position. "Ten miles?" he estimated aloud.

The skipper nodded. Lieutenant Helms agreed.

Schramm looked at the chart and marked the location. "After the war," he said, "I want to live on these islands. It must be wonderful to have sunshine all year long. If we make it through this trip," Schramm snarled. "Why are we so far from home when the war is ending? What madman has sent us here?"

"Our beloved *Führer*," Helms said with heavy sarcasm.

Helms raised his voice in disgust. "Remember Hitler's words when he came to power: 'Give me four years and you will not recognize Germany!' He needed only a few more years to completely ruin our country."

"Germany has disappeared," Brinker said, joining the discussion. "Everything has been bombed to rubble."

"So, what are we doing here?" Schramm shouted. He looked out over the heads of his companions, his eyes sweeping over the peaceful island with a look of fury. "This is no way to fight a damn war! We could've sunk several ships already."

The skipper bent down the hatch and called: "Bosun Hartmann and *Torpedomaat* Tenner to the tower!"

A moment later the two petty officers appeared. Brinker stepped to the ack-ack guns with the four men and lowered his voice so he could not be heard by the sailors below through the open hatch. "Listen! Schramm is right. This is no way to fight a war. We don't belong here. I discovered that the signature of the *BdU* on the last three operation orders was forged. Someone from the SS staff prepared the orders and faked Godt's signature."

Schramm stared at his commander.

"How could they...?" Tenner demanded. "The *BdU* — no — I don't believe it."

"Believe it," Brinker said firmly. "I've checked and I'm positive the signatures on the orders are counterfeit."

"Turn the damned boat around and go back, skipper,"

Schramm exclaimed. "We shouldn't be here."

"It's not that simple," Brinker said, eyeing his men. "We don't have enough fuel to sail home. And I have reason to believe those containers guarded by the SS contain bacteria or viruses to be spread over America by small rockets. Krantz himself told me. The plan is to kill millions of Americans with this so-called 'Miracle Weapon' and win the war."

"Unbelievable," Schramm muttered. "The SS are pigs! Nothing but murderous, crazed pigs. We must stop them, skipper."

"I agree," Tenner said, his face pale. "My God, germ warfare! My God — they are mad!"

Brinker lowered his voice even further, his eyes on the open hatch that lead below. "Helms and Hartmann already know about the danger. Hartmann's been trying to find out how they intend to activate the containers." He looked at his boatswain. "Well?"

Hartmann nodded. "They're careful. They'll speak nothing when any of our crew are in the bow room. So I thought of taking the plug out of the voice tube when they weren't looking. At first, using the voice tube that leads from the bow room to the combat center, I could hear their voices very faintly. Then I removed the locker from beside my bunk and used a piece of 5/8-inch pipe to touch the tube as I held it to my ear. That way I could hear better. Then I told Tenner to remove our crew from the bow room on the pretext that we were having an emergency drill, and I listened again."

"Well?" Brinker demanded. "What did you hear?"

Hartmann shrugged. "Not much. It was very difficult. But they did say the word *'Weinbote'* more than once. I heard that clearly."

"Are you sure they're carrying germs in those containers?" Schramm asked. "Could there be bombs of some kind?"

Brinker waved off his question. "Go on, what else did they say? We'll try to make sense of it later. Tell me what they said."

"They talked about the *'Rakete'* and to 'raise the container'."

"Go on," Brinker urged. "I want everything you can remember."

"To 'shoot the damned thing,' but sometimes they talked about Miami."

Brinker said, "That's not enough. We have to know what they intend to do."

"First, they're carrying some kind of rocket in those containers — you know the rumors that the *Führer* is working on a super weapon that will make us invincible. The kind of weapon Lembke is always talking about. Krantz intends to launch rockets from the sea. Possibly with germs. How, I don't know, but then, nothing they've said or done, has made any sense since they came on board."

"My God," Schramm breathed. "Oh, my God!"

Tenner, the torpedo officer, looked grim. "There will be no rockets going off from this boat if I can get my hands on them. Just let me see these rockets, skipper. I'll take care of them."

Brinker sighed. "If only it were that easy. The SS are heavily armed. I have a handgun in my safe. Does anyone else have a weapon?"

"A pocket knife," Schramm said despairingly.

"A wrench." Tenner laughed hollowly. "A hammer! Whatever it takes to subdue those pigs. Let the crew at them, skipper. We'll make short work of them. We'll take them by surprise, total surprise. By the way, I think we should change Lembke from the bow room to the rear torpedo room. He is the only Nazi in the crew and the only sailor the SS men talk to."

Brinker nodded, "Move him to the rear room and keep an eye on him." He allowed himself a bitter smile. "You've seen them, Tenner. They carry guns at all times. I'm sure they would not hesitate to shoot us as we came at them one by one through the bulkhead hatch. No, we're not in any condition to wage a small war. We must outsmart them. We have only a little fuel left, we're in strange waters and on our own. Whatever decisions we make will determine the future of every man on board, so we must make the right decisions, and we must make them soon!"

There was a strained silence as the men shifted from foot to foot and stared at their *Kommandant*.

Brinker nodded in understanding. "Your minds are blank. I know exactly how you feel. However, I've been living with it a slightly longer time and have one plan, but it is risky. Since we don't have fire arms, we must think about new weapons we can use to disturb and kill them. We must think of tricks to prevent them from aiming their guns at us." He paused, as the men waited eagerly. "I'll tell you when I've planned every detail. Whatever we do, our lives will depend on the actions we take." After a short pause, Brinker turned to the boatswain, "Use the stethoscope from the medical kit instead of a pipe. You might hear better."

21. Bath, England - April 21, 1945.

Three officers in the British Navy's intelligence group overheard a radio message originated from a weak station in Germany. It was repeated every half hour and in code. The officers discussed it and decided the message was probably coming from the transmitter in the Berlin Chancellery.

The message was sent upstairs to the decoding office. Two hours later the decoders produced a garbled German text with each dot representing a letter they could not decipher:

"AN U-888 STF KRANTZ FUNK......
AUF..HO... A...ONS ...ORT NICHT
ERH...... FRAGE ... KUBA ER..ICHT......
ERWARTE EINS..Z ..PORT .. 2 STUNDEN.
..MM..."

The German gibberish was handed over to the decipher experts, who found it easy to fill in the missing letters. The translated text read:

"TO U-888 STF KRANTZ. RADIO SILENCE CANCELLED. ACTION REPORT NOT RECEIVED. QUESTION IS CUBA REACHED. EXPECT REPORT ON ACTION WITHIN TWO HOURS.
..MM.."

Gilbert Glaser, a short, heavy-set decoder with extremely thick glasses on his stubby nose, pointed with his pencil at the signature. "The name here has two letters like in Himmler, right? If it's coming from the chancellery, not Goering, not Hitler."

"Our good friend Himmler," Jim Elrod, the group leader, said, grinning.

"Can't STF be the rank of this Krantz? Isn't there a *Standartenfuehrer* in the SS?" a young decoder asked.

"Come on," another officer said. "The SS was never involved with U-boats."

"Who knows? Maybe this time?" Elrod carried the sheet to

Admiral McIntire's office.

McIntire quickly scanned the text, delighted to have his theory confirmed. "I knew Himmler was involved with this sub. He's probably on his way to Argentina and wants to save his life."

"Yes, sir," Elrod said. "Himmler is involved. But we interpret this message differently. We believe Himmler is still in Berlin, expecting Krantz to report the success of some action he's supposed to take near Cuba. Action that involves the use of a U-boat."

The admiral read the message again, this time slower. "Maybe," he admitted. "Himmler could have sent this. However, I assume this is a message meant to confuse us. Send it to the Citadel. And make a copy for the OSS fellows!"

Elrod left, had the text retyped, and dropped a copy into the mailbox of the OSS group in the same building.

As usual, whenever he and his crew cracked a code, he wondered what effect it would have on the war. He knew their work was important, but they didn't often hear results after they sent off a message. It was frustrating to know only a small part of what went on in the war offices. At least once he would have liked to hear that one of his decoding jobs had saved lives or won a battle.

22. Caribbean Sea near Jamaica - April 23, 1945.

Hartmann removed the stethoscope from the medical instrument box and discovered that it worked well when he held it against the voice tube coming from the bow room.

Now he could hear every word clearly. He showed the trick to Schramm who shared his bunk. Then he told Tenner to remove his torpedomen from the bow room and inform the SS officers that the men were needed in the rear torpedo room for three hours.

What Hartmann then heard was chilling. Fortunately, he had paper and pen handy and took as many notes as he could while holding the stethoscope in the other hand. Some of what he heard he didn't understand, but he got enough to know the submarine and its crew were in peril. He reported his findings to the skipper.

"The SS men want to bring our boat close to American cities and raise the containers. You remember, there are some beams and spindles at one side of each of the containers. They will open the cover, then shoot the rocket. They said that the SS will be the only personnel on deck. The sailors and their officers will be kept below in the boat."

"Dammit!"

"Then they talk always about Meehamee, as the Bavarians pronounce Miami. They laugh about their fantasies, people dying in their bathing suits and floating in the Gulf Stream. "

"That confirms my plan," Brinker said. "We have to kill them. Did you have some ideas about new weapons, since we don't have guns? That's important!"

23. Bath, England - April 25, 1945.

Gilbert Glaser took a radio message to his group leader Elrod. "Did we never get a message back from that U-boat?" he asked.

"No," Elrod said. "Maybe the Yanks sunk it." He grinned. "Himmler won't like that."

Aaron took a copy of the new message to the OSS mailbox and was startled to find the former message about the U-boat still there. Reluctantly, he took the old message to his superior.

Elrod cursed. Taking the message he ran upstairs to the OSS group. "Why the hell hasn't your mailbox been emptied in the last four days?" he demanded of the security sergeant. The sergeant shrugged, obviously embarrassed.

"Who's in charge here?" Elrod demanded.

"Don't know. Maybe Jim." The sergeant turned in his chair. "Jim, come here!" Jim, a stooped man in his sixties, shuffled through the open door. "Jim, where is the courier?" the sergeant asked.

"He's been sick all week."

The sergeant looked at Elrod. "That explains it then."

Elrod took a deep breath. "A message from Himmler has been lying in your mailbox for four days! Do you suppose it could be of any interest to your superiors?"

"Himmler?" the sergeant repeated blankly. "The German bloke?"

Elrod exploded, describing the sergeant and his ancestors in unflattering terms, questioning the sergeant's reliability. When he had run out of adjectives, he left the room and went straight to the OSS office manager, Lt. Robertson, a slender men with an extremely thin moustache and black, shiny hair. Elrod shoved both decoded messages at the lieutenant.

"This first one has been sitting in your bloody mail box four days because a courier is sick and no one else had enough initiative to check the bloody box!"

Surprised at Elrod's anger, Lt.Robertson scanned the message.

"Oh, oh, must be Jones' sub. What the hell is it doing in Cuba? I thought it was supposed to fire a rocket on New York."

Still seething, Elrod followed the lieutenant to Jones' office where Robertson handed the message about the U-boat to the colonel.

Jones quickly read it. "This is four days old!" his face reddened with anger. "Where's it been?"

Robertson explained about the sick courier.

"Damn it! You could've done it yourself!" Jones shouted. "This is top priority, Lieutenant. Radio that information *immediately* to the Washington office, copies to Bill Donovan and Erik Svensen!"

Robertson saluted smartly. "Right away, sir!"

Jones glared at the lieutenant's back as he left the room. "How am I supposed to win a war with personnel like that?"

Elrod knew better than to answer. What might be the consequence of such negligence? he pondered.

24. Washington, D.C. - April 25, 1945.

"Bill Donovan here. Admiral Burger, please. It's urgent."

"Burger speaking."

"All hell's broken loose. The damned U-boat is going to Cuba!"

"How do you know?"

"The British intercepted a radio message from Himmler canceling the sub's radio silence. Himmler's got ants in his pants. He wants to hear from the sub and he wants to hear *now*. He's asking about the 'action off Cuba.'"

"Action off *Cuba*?"

"That's what the message says, sir. I'm sending a copy to your office. I don't think they would go to Cuba if they're planning to use rockets. It would be simpler to stay to the north and hit New York. This throws a whole new light on the sub's mission, doesn't it?"

"It looks like your theory about germ warfare may be correct. What happens if they dump something lethal into the waters off Cuba? Would it float north to our coast?"

"It's possible. They could use the Gulf Stream. But that seems too simple. It's hard to believe."

For the next fifteen seconds neither man spoke.

Finally Burger broke the silence. "I'll send everybody south. Maybe we can catch this sub before it takes action near Cuba."

Donovan cleared his throat. "There was a snafu in England, Admiral. The message is dated the 21st. It's four days old."

"Good God, Bill, that U-boat could be unloading right this minute! Get off the line! I have to make calls."

"Yes, sir...and good luck!"

25. On board U-888 - April 27, 1945.

Willy Wiener, youngest of the six SS officers, could see that his boss, *Standartenführer* Krantz, was becoming more tense as they neared Cuba. Willy, sitting in his underpants below the ventilator outlet in a vain effort to find relief from the humid heat, mopped the sweat off his body with his undershirt. Only loosely connected to the deployment of the miracle weapon, he felt no tension and was relaxed. His main job was to protect the five SS officers with his assault gun and hand grenades still hidden in the crates.

Krantz had gone to the skipper to demand the crew leave the bow room a second time so he could have another practice-run of the deployment procedure.

The torpedomen were ordered out of the bow room.

"Is the door locked?" Krantz demanded.

"Yes, *Standartenführer*," Tauber answered.

"Check it, Steltner! We must have absolute privacy."

Tauber's Adam's apple moved up and down in protest, but he remained silent.

Steltner walked to the bulkhead door. "Yes, sir. The door is locked."

Wiener mused about Krantz's continuous hostility toward Tauber. Did Tauber remind him of Hitler with his short, square moustache?

"We'll go through the operation once more," Krantz said, ignoring the weary faces of his companions. "It is vital that it runs like clockwork. We can't allow any errors."

The SS men took turns explaining what they would do, how they would go on deck, take off the deck plate above one cylindrical container and erect it by turning the spindles. Then they would open the container and shoot the first rocket against an American city to carry the war head with its content, spreading it over the population. Krantz continued to test the assignments of each one. Wiener found it all terribly boring.

"The rehearsal is over," Krantz declared at last. He turned to
Steltner. "Don't forget the briefcase should the crew make
difficulties after the deployment of all rockets."

"Yes, sir. Don't forget the briefcase. Got it."

"The rehearsal is over. Steltner, open the door!"

Wiener pondered why they picked him for this damned job.
He had been too short for the *Leibstandarte*, Hitler's troop of tall
body guards. Instead, they sent him to serve in concentration
camps. What did Krantz expect from him? To be a tough guy,
to kill even German sailors if necessary, as he had done with
Poles and Jews in the Ukraine?

26. Hohenlychen, Northern Germany - April 27, 1945.

Reichsführer SS Heinrich Himmler had left the chancellery in Berlin and established his staff headquarters in Hohenlychen, a small town north of Berlin.

Himmler had an uneasy feeling. Several months ago, Hitler had made him commander-in-chief of all German troops at the Eastern front. But, since he was unable to stop the thrust of the Soviet troops, the *Führer* had replaced him by an unknown general as commander-in-chief of the Eastern Armies. Another setback for him was Hitler's recent fury at the news that several SS generals had pulled back their Weapon-SS troops from the communist armies instead of letting them fight to the last man. Hitler had yelled that he had lost trust in the famous SS troops. This meant indirectly that he had lost trust in his SS *Reichsführer*, too. Hitler hadn't spoken to him for the last five days.

Himmler talked to *Sturmbannführer* Gockel, one of the three dedicated SS officers who still stayed with him. Gockel, a tall man who liked to show off the Knight's Cross around his neck, asked about Hitler's birthday celebration in the *Führerbunker* in Berlin.

"A sad affair," Himmler said in a low voice. "Only Hitler's closest friends and aides were there, toasting him and the Final Victory. I'd hoped to give him the news of the success of *OPERATION FEUER ALARM* as a birthday present. But this damned Krantz didn't report from Cuba."

Gockel nodded. "The people need to hear something about the V-3. Their only hope is the Miracle Weapon. So far, Goebbels has used the rumor mill very well."

Anger rose in Himmler. He had expected to be promoted to *SS Reichs Marschall* in a glorious celebration of the launching of the weapon. But his hourly repeated radio message to Krantz had not been answered. Why? What had happened to U-888?

"Why did we send the U-boat to *Cuba*?" Gockel asked. "Why didn't we attack at first in Canada and then go south?"

111

HITLER'S LAST GASP

"Two reasons. First, I was told up north were too many anti-submarine forces. Almost all U-boats in that region had recently been destroyed. It seemed to be wiser to begin in the south. Second, the scientists explained the organisms would be more active in hot and humid areas. Success could be guaranteed in those regions. I myself made the decision to begin with attacking Miami. I changed the order in the last days before the U-boat left."

"The right decision, *Reichsführer*." Gockel nodded.

Himmler was used to this reaction. All officers who had voiced another opinion had been removed from the staff. But suddenly he had some doubts.

Should I have sent the U-boat first to north-American ports? No! he thought, I never make mistakes.

Himmler reflected on the good times he had as one of Hitler's oldest friends. In 1933, after Hitler came to power, he became Chief of Police and the GESTAPO. He built concentration camps and arrested millions of Germans for the smallest signs of disagreement with the N.S. party line. Governing a nation by terror, creating fear, that was his maxim. He knew it would work. He also masterminded the mass-killing of Jews in extermination camps in Poland.

Now, most of Germany occupied by the enemy, and seeing himself without a leadership task, he felt abandoned by the *Führer* who had decided to stay in Berlin. He wanted to survive and had taken the initiative to arrange a truce with American and British forces without Hitler's knowledge. He was convinced that the strange alliance between the western powers and the communists would disintegrate soon and end up in open hostility. He had offered to lead the SS troops for fighting with the Western Allied armies against Stalin and to smash communism. He had contacted Count Bernadotte, the Red Cross director from Sweden, as a middleman on April 21 and two days later dined with him in secrecy in Lübeck, a Baltic seaport.

With utmost clarity Himmler remembered their conversation. Bernadotte wanted proof that Himmler was still in charge of the police, the SS and German troops. "Of course I am." Himmler squared his shoulders. "What do you want done?"

"Redirect to Sweden the 3,000 American and British prisoners marching west in Mecklenburg. The Jewish people on their way to a concentration camp in Southern Germany, let them emigrate to Switzerland."

Himmler called his aide, *Standartenführer* Fegelein, Eva Braun's brother-in-law. "Arrange for the Allied prisoners, who are marching to the west, to be sent directly to Sweden! Then redirect the 4,000 Jews on their way to concentration camps to Switzerland instead! Without delay!"

Turning back to the count, he asked: "Does that satisfy you?"

"I'll be satisfied only when I receive verification that your orders have been followed and these people have left Germany."

Now, left to wait, he could only hope the trick would work. On his order several thousand prisoners were transported to Sweden and thousands of Jewish men, women and children were allowed to pass the border into Switzerland. But still no response from the count on his proposal to the American and British supreme commanders to make a special peace arrangement with him as the new German *Führer*. But Bernadotte had not called him. He wondered why?

Unaccustomed to waiting, he paced up and down his office. Finally, he opened his door and stepped into the large room outside his office. Rage overcame him when he saw his staff members lounging in armchairs, their jackets open, their booted legs stretched wide. Unable to control himself he shouted: "Why does Krantz not report to me? Why must I wait for his message? If he were here I would order him shot on the spot."

His staff, used to taking the blame for others' shortcomings, jumped from their chairs, buttoned their jackets and kept silent. They stood at attention, staring at him with stern faces.

He pulled himself together. "Connect me with Bormann!" he ordered.

One tall officer clicked his heels and cranked up the nearest field telephone, trying to get through to the *Führerbunker*. It took several minutes, during which Himmler drummed his fingers on the table.

Another SS officer spoke. "May I ask permission to report to *Reichsführer* that the British announced that 62 of our U-boats have been sunk this month? Maybe *Standartenführer* Krantz has died in honor of our *Führer* and Fatherland."

"How did you get this defeatist information? Do you listen to enemy radio stations? You'll be — "

"Martin Bormann on the line, sir," the tall officer said.

Himmler took the telephone. "Bormann?" He raised his voice as he heard static on the line. "Is this Martin Bormann? Speak louder! ...I can't hear you... Bormann? ...Finally. Did you get a report from Krantz? ...You didn't? How do you explain this? ... I can't understand you. Speak louder!"

He turned and saw his staff members staring at him. "*Raus!*" he yelled at them.

Instantly they left.

"Hello! Bormann? ... Can't hear you. Speak louder! ...How's Hitler? ... Desperate? ... He bit rugs again? ... How's Eva? Is she with him? ... That damned whore! ... Why haven't we heard from U-888? Krantz will be shot when he's back!...." Click. "Hello, Bormann? ... Hello! ... Bormann?"

Himmler threw the phone on the floor.

"The bastard hung up on me!"

The telephone rang. He picked it up, surprised that it still worked. "Bormann?"

"No, this is Bernadotte."

"Count Bernadotte?"

"Yes. Am I speaking with *Reichsführer SS* Himmler?"

"Yes, Himmler speaking." He straightened, his mind racing with possibilities.

"Can you understand me?"

"Yes, I hear you loud and clear."

"I contacted General Montgomery and General Eisenhower. Both generals reject your offer and declare it unacceptable."

"Whaaat?"

"There is no way the Americans will make a separate agreement without the Soviet Union."

"What? They have rejected *my* offer? They are mad! We will be slaughtered! You must speak to them again!"

"Herr Himmler, your offer is unacceptable."

"No, it can't be. My offer is ..."

Click. The line went dead.

Himmler smashed the phone against the wall, hammering it to pieces, and stormed out of the antechamber to the street. "Gockel, prepare all cars and trucks! We leave this place in ten minutes. We'll drive north. *Schnell, schnell!*"

Deep inside, Himmler knew he had lost. The trip north might put off the inevitable for a few days, but there was no place to hide. Everyone failed him. Through no fault of his, the *Reich* would go down in defeat. His and Hitler's dreams were over.

In the small building most staff members busied themselves packing. Himmler stepped out of the building and paced up and down in the court. He watched as an Army sergeant drove away with one of the jeeps toward the south.

"Who was that?" he asked a truck driver.

"*Sturmbannführer* Gockel. He loaded two extra gas tanks."

For a while Himmler was silent. He looked down at the dirty floor. Then he said, "We'll drive north."

27. Near Cape San Antonio, Cuba - April 30, 1945.

Heading north, U-888 reached Cape San Antonio, the westernmost point of Cuba, at six in the morning, almost a month after leaving Wilhelmshaven. It sailed around the promontory into the current of the Gulf Stream that flowed between Cuba and the United States.

At dawn Boatswain Hartmann stood on the conning tower. During the last week he'd thought about the skipper's plan to end the SS officers' mission. When he himself suggested the code name FRIED CHICKEN for the plan, everyone grinned. Still the officers were convinced the very detailed plan would work.

Coming down into the boat, Hartmann sensed tension on the crew's faces. "We'll get fried chicken for breakfast," quipped Schramm, the navigator.

Hartmann's stomach tightened as he realized that soon FRIED CHICKEN would either liberate the crew or annihilate them. He saw Schramm and three others throwing knives against a package of linen, bundled up like a human figure, where two knives already stuck. "Uhuh! Trying the new weapons?"

On Brinker's orders, Helms took all submarine officers and *Standartenführer* Krantz to the wardroom. Brinker informed the SS leader that the U-boat had reached Quadrant DM 3300, the location assigned in the last order.

"Got suddenly some extra fuel, hey?" Krantz asked.

"Favorable currents pushed the boat ahead. Can I get the envelope with the next order?"

Obviously surprised, Krantz pulled his fingers. His eyes wandered from one officer to the next.

Finally he stood up and straightened his body to its full length. "I want my four officers here from the bow room," he said to the *Kommandant*.

Brinker sent the boatswain to the bow room. "Hand Tenner the torpedo oil he wanted." He passed an oil can from the shelf to

Hartmann.

After the boatswain came back with the four black-clad officers, Krantz glanced at all naval and SS officers who were crowded into the small officers' wardroom. Then he spoke with a loud voice, staring at the *Kommandant.* "There are no more written instructions for you. From now on *I* take command of the U-boat. First, I order you to sail the boat to a point exactly ten miles south of Miami. Understand?!" His hateful stare swept over the officers, coming to rest on the skipper's stern face. "Second: All crew members evacuate the bow room for *my* officers right now!"

Controlled, Brinker spoke over the intercom: "*Torpedomaat* Tenner and all personnel in the bow room come to the combat center!"

Krantz's face showed contentment. "This boat is under command of the National Socialist Party and the SS. Understand? As representative of *Reichsführer* Himmler, I'll lead this boat to fight for the Thousand-year German *Reich.* From now on, I insist, every order must be obeyed exactly. At noon, the officers will change rooms. Naval officers to the bow room, SS to the officers' wardroom. You'll get further orders from me soon. Report to me when you've reached the new position. Heil Hitler!" His arm shot out swift and straight, then he turned, gestured to his men to go to the bow room and followed them stiffly through the boat.

Hartmann's heart beat rapidly. He had expected something like this to happen, but was horrified when it did. This was open war of the Nazis against the *Kriegsmarine!* This was treason! He left the room ahead of the SS officers.

He heard confused yelling from the bow section. "Sorry," Tenner's voice sounded above trampling steps of the sailors. "The oil can slipped from me. Sorry."

"Take care!" "Don't step on my hands! Idiot!" Sailors shouted, falling on the slippery deck.

In the combat center, Brinker ordered, "A-group on deck, quickly! B-group on stand-by!" The order was forwarded from man to man. They rushed toward the conning tower and climbed the ladder to the turret, then jumped on deck.

As planned, Lieutenant Helms followed Krantz who was the last of the SS men. They made their way through the bow room crew who hastened to the combat center.

While Helms accepted Tenner's report "All Navy personnel have left the bow room," Hartmann saw how Krantz squeezed through the round hatch into the bow room and yelled back to Helms, "I'll have a meeting with my personnel. This hatch is to stay closed, understood?"

"Yessir. I'll take care of it personally." Helms closed the hatch, rotated the lock and put a crow bar through the lock handle, blocking any movement of it. With arm raised and fist closed, Helms signaled the lock-up to his skipper.

Hartmann connected the stethoscope to the voice tube in the combat center to listen to the sounds from the bow room:

"What happened?" he heard Krantz shout. "What's this slippery stuff here?"

"Tenner dropped the oil can," Wiener responded.

"You asshole!" Steltner yelled, "Oooohey! We can't stand here. Clean that damned floor!"

Tauber yelled, "Why didn't you take care, Wiener? We can't walk here."

Helms poised for his prepared speech over the intercom, blaring through all rooms.

"*Achtung*! As executive officer I'm responsible for order and safety on this boat. The *Kommandant* is entirely in command on a U-boat. Only *he* has the right to carry a pistol on board. Anyone else with a gun is a mutineer."

Hartmann heard Krantz yell, "*I'*m in command here! *Aufmachen*! Open the bulkhead!"

Helms continued, "Krantz has tried to seize power. He smuggled weapons on board. He destroyed our radio equipment."

Hartmann called to the skipper, "Krantz shouted, 'I had to, you hooligans!'"

Helms continued, over the intercom, "This is mutiny! I order the SS to hand over all firearms. I give you ten seconds or you'll be killed. I'm counting: one ... two ... three...."

Brinker went to Hartmann's side and put one end of the stethoscope into his ear. He then ordered over the intercom, "Both diesels full speed ahead! Deck crew, prepare to open torpedo hatch! Ready for action!"

"Four ..." Helms counted.

"We'll massacre these pigs!" Krantz yelled. "I'll shoot them all."

"Five ..." Helms counted.

Several SS men banged against the bulkhead. "*Aufmachen!* You traitors! You damned fags." Hell broke loose in the bow room. Hartmann could hear how they slipped and fell to the deck, shouting angry curses.

Krantz roared, "Tenner! Obey my order: Kill the *Kommandant!* Kill Helms!"

"Six..." Helms counted.

"Steltner," Krantz shouted. "Get the grenades!"

"Seven ... eight .."

Suddenly Krantz yelled: "*Halt!* I'll hand over the weapons. We must fulfill our mission! We must deploy the weapon!"

Brinker grabbed the microphone. "Your weapon will *not* be deployed. You forged the *BdU's* signature on the operation orders. Hand over your arms — *now!*"

"Pig!" Krantz thundered. "Let's blow up the boat."

"Nine ... ten." Helms counted.

Brinker ordered, "Rudder hard starbord!"

The boat trembled as the diesel engines roared at full speed and the propellers gave their best output. The boat leaned sharply toward port side. Hartmann thought, all SS men must now lose their grip and slide through the slippery bow room over the vibrating deck plates. The A-crew on the upper deck opened the slanted torpedo hatch and locked it in open position. Tenner, kneeling beside the hatch where he was protected against bullets from the SS men, held a mirror attached to a bar over the open hatch. Through the mirror he saw the SS officers sliding and tumbling over the slippery slanted deck. Total chaos below! Still, one of them, squeezed between the torpedo tubes, held a gun and aimed at the mirror.

Sklirrrrr. The mirror was hit, broken glass flew through the air over deck where the sailors of the A-group stood, ready for action. Several bullets flew through the open hatch over the conning tower. The sailors threw themselves down on the deck.

Brinker commanded, "Rudder hard port side!"

Loud yelling came from the bow room. They seemed to slide over the oily deck. Krant'z voice, "Throw it, asshole!"

A grenade fell on deck, rolled over the wooden planks, its ignition end sizzling. A sailor jumped and pushed it wide over board.

Pong! It exploded under water. A pile of water beamed up besides the boat twenty feet above the surface, then collapsed in itself. The boat's hull shook like a drum's skin, sounding as if being hit by a giant sledge hammer.

Brinker yelled. "These assholes want to blow us up! Use water!"

Machinists of the B-group rushed forward. Two of them held the nozzle of the water hose. A sharp stream of piercing water was directed through the hatch against the SS officers.

"Rudder hard starbord!" Brinker ordered.

Tenner held another mirror over the hatch, saw the SS men sliding and falling over each other in the room below. The oil made the SS men desperate and unable to act. The machinists swung the powerful water stream back and forth into the bow room, hitting the SS men again and again. Desperate yelling came from below. The water stream was an effective weapon, allowing no defense against it in the small room. Unaimed bullets whirled through the bow room. Some flew through the hatch above the deck. Another grenade fell on deck and came to rest besides the machinists at the nozzle. A sailor jumped forward, grabbed the grenade and threw it back into the hatch.

Pong! It exploded in the bow room. Black and brown powder

smoke blew out of the hatch opening over deck. The machinists were pushed back with their nozzle to the side. The yelling of injured SS men could be heard. Engineer Borger jumped forward, stood for a moment close to the hatch and whirled a heavy knife down through the opening. It hit Tauber's face right besides his Hitler-like moustache. He fell down and slid to the bulkhead. Schramm jumped forward and hurled his knife into Tauber's chest.

"Arrrughhh", sounded from below, then a splash of a falling body. A burst of an assault gun, triggered by a wounded SS officer. The bullets of that round ricocheted in the boat. Only two bullets came through the hatch. Other shots from below with an assault gun hit the hull. Borger fired the next knife at an SS officer, a sailor threw a wrench down, hitting the collapsing SS man with full power at his head. Both felled him, and the water stream washed him below the torpedo tubes. Loud yelling of wounded men came from below.

Now Helms had opened the bulkhead hatch inside the boat, stormed into the room and threw a crow bar like a spear against an SS man who stood in the front corner. His body collapsed like a slaughtered ox. At this moment, the boat tilted again. Helms had wire woven around his shoes to prevent him from sliding. The short wire ends stuck in the small deck holes and gave him firm support. In contrast, the SS man were constantly sliding when pushed by the sharp stream of water. Radioman Abert, at Helms's side, had a knife in his hand. With a short stroke he sent the blade flying through the room. It was aimed at the short-bodied Willy Wiener, lying on the deck and shooting his assault gun through the open hatch. The pointed knife hit him in the throat below his chin. His head fell heavily to the side like a rock. The gun still in his hand spread ten more shots against the bunk beds in the room. Abert saw Schmidt aiming a gun at him. He whirled a second knife through the air, hit Schmidt's head between the eyes. Blood splashed around his mutilated head.

Helms saw Krantz lying on the deck, half-covered by the

bench, hands below the deck plates. "Krantz!" Helms shouted, "Hands up!" Helms stepped forward, yelled to the people on deck, "Stop water! It's over!" He ripped Krantz's arm up, saw he was bleeding, his face blackened from the powder of the grenade that exploded in the bow room. "Get up, you pig!"

The bow room was devastated. The grenade had ripped apart everything. Table, benches, bunks and bed sheets were a shambles, lockers bent to irregular shapes.

Suddenly Krantz collapsed on the deck.

Helms went from body to body, looking carefully at them, kicking each with his foot. "All dead. Hand me a rope!" he shouted to the sailors above. They threw one down and three sailors who had followed Helms into the bow room, tied it around Krantz's unconscious body. Sailors hauled him on deck. The five dead bodies followed and were laid out on deck.

Brinker ordered "Diesels half speed. Rudder midships!" He stepped down from the conning tower and looked at the dead SS men. He saw Krantz who seemed to regain consciousness.

Slowly Krantz got up, stumbled and fell. "You bastards!" he yelled, fury lighting up his face. "You've destroyed Germany, you traitors!" He fell again and crawled over the deck on all fours, wearing only his underpants and covering his body with his black uniform jacket. "You'll pay for this." Exhausted he fell down again.

Brinker went from body to body.

He confronted Krantz. "Now will you tell me about your plan? What were you going to do with this boat?"

"My plan?" Krantz answered bitterly. "It was to destroy the world around Germany." The SS leader jumped up and lunged angrily toward the *Kommandant*.

In that moment, Helms stepped forward, punched Krantz in his face, pushing him forcefully back so that he fell and rolled overboard. With a splash his body disappeared over the side of the boat which was cutting at eight knots through the water.

"Krantz, the mass murderer, will drown," Helms said.

Kapitänleutnant Brinker ordered the five dead SS men to be thrown overboard. "Tie something heavy to their bodies! They don't deserve an honorable burial," he said. "They not only wanted to kill millions of people but intended also to destroy us and our boat. Now we'll clean up. The bosun and *Torpedomaat* Tenner take charge in the bow room; Lieutenant Helms takes charge on deck!"

The SS men's belongings were thrown overboard. Each splash of the black uniforms, boots and kit bags was applauded by the sailors. Within seconds the waves gobbled up all Nazi paraphernalia.

In the shattered torpedo room blood had spattered everywhere and had to be washed away. Parts of the wooden overhead had fallen down and had to be placed in position again. Bed sheets needed to be washed and dried, personal belongings of the crew put back into lockers, and light bulbs replaced. Tenner and Hartmann checked the room for damage. Hartmann thought, what a group of strange fanatics! After hours of work, *Torpedomaat* Tenner reported to the skipper on deck. "*Herr Kaleu*, the torpedo room is as squared away as we can make it."

"*Danke*," Brinker said. "I want to see it." Both climbed down into the boat.

The skipper turned to Tenner. "Did you make sure *all* their stuff is gone? Remember what they said when they rehearsed their deployment procedure?

"Yes, sir." Tenner said. "But — did we bring the briefcase on deck?"

"Yes, we did," a seaman said.

"But that was the *brown* briefcase with the documents," another mechanic said, "not the *black* one. We put the brown one back into the officer's wardroom."

Turning to Tenner, Brinker said, "Search for the black one!" Looking at Hartmann he asked, "Hartmann, What's in it?"

"No idea, *Herr Kaleu*. I only remember Krantz talked about it."

The men turned everything upside down, but found nothing.

"Keep searching," Brinker said.

Deep in thoughts the *Kommandant* walked through the boat to the officers' wardroom.

Radio operator Abert approached the skipper. "*Herr Kaleu*, I finished a transmitter for Morse code signals. I'm still working on a small receiver."

"What's its range?" Brinker asked.

"Twenty to thirty miles."

"Good enough for a call on Cuba. I'll write a message for you to try out. Get going with the receiver."

"I'm almost done, *Herr Kaleu*. I'm already testing it."

On the way to his office nook, Brinker tried to come up with a far-reaching decision. Surrender he must. To the Americans? They'd shoot his boat down before he could even explain. To the Cubans? They had no anti-sub forces. It might be the best solution. He composed a short text, then called for Abert to broadcast it.

When he returned to the conning tower the second watch officer reported, "Small fishing boat at port side behind us, *Herr Kaleu*."

"Keep looking!"

Shortly after, Abert, his face pale, came up to the conning tower. "*Herr Kaleu*, I have a for-your-ears-only message."

Both went to the ack-ack platform where nobody could hear them.

"I've finished the radio receiver. It's so weak I have to use earphones. An American station said Berlin has been taken by the Russians. The *Führer* is dead. Admiral Dönitz is his successor."

28. Santa Fé, Isla de Piños, Cuba - April 30, 1945.

"Ben je't nog niet zat, Jan?" Julie van der Reems asked her husband. "Aren't you tired? How long do you plan to stay at your radio?"

Julie regarded Jan, an enthusiastic ham radio operator, with amused tolerance. The two had left Jamaica four years ago when he retired from a Dutch trading company. Now they lived on the small Cuban Isle of the Pines. The little city of Santa Fé, in the center of the flat island, was about one hundred miles south of Havana. The only connection with Cuba was by boat or telephone.

"Another ten minutes, Julie," he said. Now retired after twenty-five years of work, Jan enjoyed every hour spent on his hobby. He turned the knobs of his radio, trying to improve the reception from a weak station. He pressed the ear phones more closely to his round head, sparsely covered by blond hair.

Did he hear right? He automatically scribbled down the letters of a transmission in Morse code:

"...A N S U B M A R I N E W E A R E A G E R M A N S U B M A R I N E W E A R E ... ... " The signal weakened. Jan delicately turned the knobs.

It came in again:

" ... O N B O A R D R E P E A T H A V E L E T H A L W E A P O N O N B O A R D R E P ..." The signal faded away.

Julie stood beside him. "What country are you listening to?" she asked

"Quiet!" Jan showed his wife the letters he had jotted down. "Seems to be pure nonsense. Should I call Thornbourgh?"

"Don't call. It's a joke," Julie said with conviction.

The signal came back again:

" ... N T T O B E I N T E R N E D I N C U B A W A N T T O B E I N T E R ... ... 8 8 8 ... ...L E T H A L W E A ... ... C I E N F U E ... ..." Jan tried

everything to retrieve the signal. Wait, here it comes again:
"... S T R O P H E   D O N T   B O M B   ..." Gone
again. This time he couldn't get the signal back.

Jan looked at what he had scribbled. He noted down the
frequency and time - 1:31 p.m. - and the date - 4/30/45. Damn,
was it a crank call? Was it real or was some jerk playing a joke?

He left the radio to eat his lunch and think about the
fragmented message. Although lunch was an excellent salad with
lettuce, mushrooms, bell peppers and a hearty sandwich of ham
and eggs, he tasted none of it. When he finished, he kissed Julie
on the cheek and took a short nap.

When he woke, the first thing he thought of was the strange
message. He didn't know what to do about it. He had listened to
short radio bursts from German U-boats before and had alerted
the American communications officer at Guantánamo Bay five
separate times. His phone calls from the only phone in
downtown Santa Fé resulted in submarine hunts that destroyed
at least three U-boats. His effort had won for him the privilege
of having his own phone line strung on poles from the main line
to his house.

But this latest message was different. Reluctantly he called the
American base and after a short wait he got through to
Lieutenant Thornbourg.

"You understand, it may be a crank call," Jan said, "but I have
received a message that says it is from a German sub." He read
off the disjointed words he had copied down.

"That's a queer one," Thornbourg agreed. "Read it again,
please."

But the second reading was no clearer than the first.

"You may be right, Jan. It sure sounds like someone's having
a little fun. I'll ask around, but as far as I know there are no
more U-boats in the area. You keep listening and let me know
if you hear any more. Keep up the good work."

Jan hung up the phone slowly, wondering if Thornbourg
would take any action at all. After all, wasn't it true that the war
in Europe was coming to an end? What would a German sub be

doing in Cuban waters?

Jan, not wishing to try Julie's patience too far, strolled outside for an hour or two of work in the garden. After all, how many hours a day could a grown man spend listening to idiotic messages about subs and lethal weapons?

Jan worked in the yard and planted new seeds for vegetables until dinner time.

29. Near Cape San Antonio, Cuba - April 30, 1945.

Brinker stood on the gun platform, leaning against the railing, eyes peering down into the blue water as he adjusted to the idea that the war might soon be over. It would certainly be dangerous to sail to an American port. He ordered the third watch officer, "Dive and go to periscope depth!" The men on the conning tower went down into the boat, the Kommandant as the last. The boat now sailed under water at slow speed through the calm sea. The diesel noise gave way to the soft humming of the electromotors that pushed the submarine through the water.

When he was ready to address his men, he picked up the mike.

"Kommandant to crew: I have news for you. *Funkmaat* Abert has built a small receiver from the debris of his radio equipment. He's heard an American radio station say that the *Führer* is dead. Admiral Dönitz is Hitler's successor. According to the station, Berlin is in the hands of the Russians. I assume the war will be over within days or even hours. I have decided to surrender our boat to the Cubans. We sail to the port of Cienfuegos. End of message."

"Shame! We lost the war! All was in vain!"

"The Russians in Berlin! How is my wife? My kids?"

"*Hurra! Hurra!*" some men shouted. "The war is over! We survived!"

The men discussed the situation from many points of view. The war had stretched over six years. What would happen to their country? Would they be able to return to their homes and families?

The skipper sat down and recorded the day's events in the log book. "Müller to *Kommandant*!" he called. The short, friendly cook came instantly and stretched his body to attention, looking at his skipper.

"Everybody gets a bottle of beer from the secret box. We'll celebrate the near end of the war!"

While the submarine continued under water, the sailors sat around the tables, clinging to their beer bottles, one started singing 'Back to home'. All others joined, their thoughts flying across the Atlantic.

The officers aired their opinions in the ward room.

"Why did the SS want to sail to Cuba?" Lieutenant Topper asked.

"No idea," Brinker said. "Another brass's mistake."

"They made so many wrong decisions that we lost the war."

"The worst was to attack London instead of the British air force."

"Why did they attack the Soviets?"

"*Dummkopf*! Had we invaded England, the six million Soviet troops would have run over Germany and Western Europe."

"Why didn't they free the Ukrainians? They would have fought with us against Stalin."

"That was against the Nazis' ideology!"

"Remember, our soldiers near Moscow had no winter clothing."

"Why didn't they take Leningrad? They could've eliminated the Soviet fleet."

Brinker calmed them down: "Everybody makes mistakes. What did *we* do wrong? We fought six years in the Atlantic in vain."

"At least we kicked out the SS..."

"And we didn't blast off Hitler's miracle weapon!"

"*Herr Kaleu*, you'll get the Diamonds to the Swords of the Knight's Cross for that."

"And Roosevelt will give you the Medal of Freedom!"

Brinker lifted his hand. "I'll no longer go to sea. This is my last war. I look forward to when men will look at wars as a thing of the past, as we do now at duels."

"I'll work on my uncle's farm," Helms said. "I, too, will never go to sea again."

Engineer Borger leaned back. "I'd like to go into archeology. Go to Peru. I want to excavate Inca cities."

"Do you think people were better then? You're a dreamer.

People have always been *Dummköpfe*," Schramm said.

Borger tilted his beer bottle and drained it. "Of course, those people were more reasonable than we are today."

The skipper lifted his hand. "Humans are a destructive species. Unreasonable leaders appear in every civilization. And there are people who follow those men. Look at me. I sank thirty-nine ships and two destroyers. And why? Because a madman wanted to rule Europe. I didn't realize how mad Hitler was. It happens again and again in history. We Germans are not the only naive idealists who have gone to war for the wrong reasons. Don't forget Napoleon, who was blindly followed by the French, conquering all of Europe until he lost in Moscow."

"I'll emigrate to Chile," the third officer said. "My sister lives over there."

"Not me!" the chief engineer exclaimed. "The only thing I want to do is go to bed with my wife for a week. For a whole week! And do what I missed all these years. Do you hear me? A whole week naked in bed with her!"

"*Kommandant* to the command center," blared over the intercom. Brinker looked at his wristwatch. 15:12. He stood up and went to the periscope room.

"Fishing boat coming closer at 150 degrees, *Herr Kaleu*," said the third watch officer.

The *Kommandant* looked through the periscope. He rotated it for a total sweep around. "Did you see that white yacht ahead of us? Still far away." He took the helm. Nodding at the officer and the helmsman he said, "You go down and celebrate. You deserve your beer. Send Helms up in five minutes to relieve you."

The second watch officer and the helmsman descended and joined the noisy crew. The *Kommandant* was alone in the upper command room. He enjoyed it, not being looked up to for a moment by his officers or men. Where was Ursula and their daughter now? Irmgard was so cute. Were they safe in Kiel or were they sent to the country side? He hadn't seen or spoken to his wife for one month! When would he see her again?

Brinker noticed that the noise below ended abruptly. The

helmsman appeared below in the command center, bottle in hand, trembling. Then he saw Engineer Borger, staring up at him. "Everyone is dying! We're pois...." He collapsed with a horrified look on his distorted face.

Brinker was stunned. What could it be? Why this sudden silence? He smelled a metallic odor. The briefcase? He knelt down, dropped the hatch at his feet and was thus separated from the lower rooms. He became drowsy. I've got to get out of here, if I want to stay alive!

He activated the switch to release the rubber boat they once had installed to bring three spies ashore at Canada. Then he pushed the lever for the emergency weight that dropped and let the boat rise to the surface. He had asked for it to raise the boat without using the noisy air system. Pain threatened to burst his lungs. With an extreme effort he turned the wheel of the upper hatch. He used his last strength to open it and crawl out. On the conning tower he collapsed.

Without guidance, the submarine went down again. Water splashed over the turret deck, pushed the *Kommandant* away from the turret and streamed into the periscope room. Brinker stirred and then quickly swam to the small black-painted rubber boat the wind threatened to blow away from him.

Krantz's sinister plot to poison the crew by hiding the briefcase filled with two deadly chemicals had worked. He had placed the briefcase under the deckplates and activated the timer before surrendering.

The driverless U-boat sank slowly to the sea floor. The dead crew lay scattered on bunks, on the deck, at their diving stations. Eventually, the electromotors stopped running and there were no more engine sounds. Only the sighing of the sea remained.

Himmler's miracle weapon now lay with the dead of U-888 near the Isle of Pines off Cuba's coast. Hitler was defeated, dead. Yet his 'Miracle Weapon' survived, waiting for the proper trigger to spread its lethal load.

30. Santa Fé, Isla de Piños, Cuba - May 1, 1945.

During the night, Jan van der Reems was awakened by the continuous ringing of his telephone. He looked at his alarm clock. 2:30 in the morning. Someone ringing the wrong number, he assumed. When it didn't stop, he got up and answered it.

"*Aló*! Jan?"

"*Quién*?"

"I want to talk to Jan van der Reems."

"Speaking."

"Lieutenant Thornbourg from the base. A moment please, Admiral Curtis wants to speak with you."

There was a loud click that almost broke his eardrum. "Admiral Curtis here. I'm sorry to call you in the middle of the night. You reported a strange message to Lieutenant Thornbourg. Could you please repeat the message for me? I think it might be real."

"Just a minute." He rooted through the wastepaper basket until he found the crumpled sheet of paper with his notes about the German sub. He read it to the admiral. Then he mentioned the time he took the message and the frequency he used.

"Thank you, Mr. van der Reems. Please, excuse the interruption of your sleep. This is indeed a strange message. If you should hear more from the German sub, call Lieutenant Thornbourg immediately. Good night."

Julie was angry. "I don't want a phone in the house if it's going to wake us up at night."

"That was the admiral from the base. A most important call."

"Why are you putting on your pants? Where are you going?"

"I think I'll listen to my radio. I don't want to miss anything important."

"You're crazy." His wife turned her back to him.

"Perhaps. In fact, it's quite possible, but I'll listen for a while. You never know what you'll hear."

31. OSS Office, Washington, D.C. - May 1, 1945.

"Russ Bender?"

"Bender speaking."

"Admiral Burger calling."

The phone clicked twice.

"Burger here. We've received a strange message from Guantánamo Base. Do you hear me?"

"Loud and clear."

"A U-boat sent a radio message in open Morse code, saying it has a lethal weapon on board and wants to surrender. It identified itself as U-888. That must be FIRE ALARM. A copy of the crippled message is on its way to you."

"Good God! Do you suppose...."

"If we're lucky, this is the one we're looking for. I've re-issued the order to not attack U-boats in our southern region. We don't want any foul-ups now."

"Affirmative."

"Call me as soon as you read the message. Out."

Russ Bender dialed Erik's number.

"Erik, FIRE ALARM radioed it wants to surrender. Come and see me. We have to make decisions."

32. Near Isla de Piñas - May 1, 1945.

After a desperate effort to reach the small rubber boat, that the wind was blowing away from him, the skipper of U-888 climbed onto his new vessel. He lay down exhausted and looked into the endless blue space above him. He was in heavy shock. He had lost his U-boat and his crew! All his men were dead. He was a *Kommandant* without a boat!

What had he done wrong? The last six hours were an uninterrupted sequence of actions to get rid of the SS intruders, ending in a celebration of the news of the soon to be expected end of the war. Had he been negligent? Did gases come from the battery? No, the battery wasn't charged. Or was the black briefcase the source of deadly gases? He had once been told that the SS used poisonous gases in small packages to kill Soviet commissars in barrack buildings in the Ukraine. Should he have insisted on searching for the black briefcase? Hartmann had reported that Krantz mentioned the briefcase several times to Steltner. So it must have been an important tool in Krantz's hands.

Brinker became aware that he had overwhelmed the SS men on his U-boat, but the mysterious miracle weapon with its terrible load of dangerous microorganisms was still on the boat. Its threat against humanity did still exist! It was now *his* duty to alert the world and do something to make it harmless. He had to survive! He had to row to the Cuban coast. How far was it? He lifted himself in his black boat and saw the coast as a grayish line in the north, five, maybe ten miles distant. He couldn't estimate any better. When he looked around, he saw the white sails of a yacht only a few miles away from him. He hoped it would come closer to pick him up.

33. Along the Cuban coast - May 1, 1945.

Four women were sailing west along the Cuban coast, spending their vacations on a light-blue pleasure yacht. Murphy Andrews, an American woman and her three Latin American friends, wanted to enjoy two weeks on a boat that could sleep up to six persons. Since all fighting men had gone with their vessels or airplanes to the north for a U-boat hunt, the four young ladies, working in U.S Navy offices, had little to do and were sent on vacation. They had a wonderful time, hoping the war would be over when their furlough ended and a wave of new activities would begin.

Since no German ships had been seen in the Carribean in the last few months, sailing from Guantánamo Naval Base westward to Havana was no longer considered dangerous. Murphy had planned to sail to Havana and stay there for a week before returning to Guantánamo where she worked as secretary for the base administrator. Good family connections helped her get this job of little responsibility but good pay. Amanda, Maria and Sylvia were her colleagues at the base.

The four young women played bridge on deck and sipped their Martinis. Murphy, a woman with shoulder-length blond hair, was at the helm.

"What's that black stuff over there? See it?" Murphy pointed to port side.

Amanda looked through her binoculars. "Strange. why don't you get closer?"

The three showed little interest and continued playing bridge. After a while Amanda took her binoculars again. "It looks as if a guy's rowing there," she called.

Murphy turned the boat around. As she came nearer, she said, "He's trying to paddle away from us!" and followed him, reducing the distance slowly. The four women saw to their surprise that the man undressed, and threw a light brown shirt overboard.

Half an hour later, the four hauled a tall blond man, about thirty, on board. He lay down on deck and closed his eyes, seemed unable to speak. He was clothed only in his short pants, nothing else. Murphy noticed he wasn't sunburnt. "He looks strong. But isn't it strange that he isn't tanned?"

"How in the world did he end up here?" Amanda asked. "He's half dead."

"He's exhausted from rowing." Sylvia said.

Maria checked the man's vital signs. "His pulse is okay and he's breathing. But very slowly. Who knows how long he's been floating here? Is he ship-wrecked?"

"Let's get him into the cabin where there's shade," Murphy said.

It wasn't easy to bring him down through the narrow and steep staircase. Maria put a soft cushion under his head and checked his eyes. "He's still alive, but very weak."

"What do we do? Where can we get help? He needs a doctor," Amanda said.

"The closest port is Cienfuegos," Murphy suggested.

The four women tried to get the stranger to speak, asking him in English, "Do you want something to drink? Are you hungry?"

He shook his head slowly.

"What's your name?"

He didn't answer.

"Do you understand English? *Habla español*?"

No answer.

They tried to communicate with the man in vain for half an hour until they heard him whisper, "I don't remember."

"He speaks English!" Murphy said, looking at her friends.

They renewed their efforts to find out where he came from, and his nationality. His English had a strong foreign accent, Scandinavian or Dutch. But they heard nothing more than, "I don't know," or, "I don't remember."

Murphy said, "Has he been in an accident? Did he fall overboard from his ship?"

"For sure he's suffering from amnesia," Maria said. "Poor

fellow! What might have happened to him? We must get him ashore and to a doctor."

"But not to a hospital! It's so primitive. We should find him a better stay," Sylvia said. "Don't send him to a government facility."

"Let's call Michele. She may help us," Murphy said. "She's in her summer home in Cienfuegos. She has a car and can take him to a place where he can recover."

In the early evening hours they landed in Cienfuegos where Murphy called Michele. She came to the pier and took the stranger to her summer house in the vicinity of Cienfuegos. "I'll see what I can do for him," Michele said. "At first he may stay in my bungalow." When they finally reached their destination, the stranger was still reluctant to speak. "I don't remember," was all he could say.

Michele gave him a shirt and pajamas, then left the room to prepare something to eat. When she came with a tray with food and a drink, she found him lying in the guest bed fully asleep, snoring softly. She looked at him, brushed his hair, and wondered where he came from. She found him good-looking and well-built, his face showing sophistication. She prayed that he would get better soon. Her tongue glided across her lips.

34. Near Cienfuegos - Cuba May 2, 1945.

Hans Brinker opened his eyes and found himself in a wide bed in an unfamiliar room with small windows. This was not his bedroom at home. The small windows allowed him to see a blue sky. He looked at his arm. It was wrapped in some pink material. So was his other arm. He threw back his cover and stared at the rest of himself. He wore pink pajamas! What in the hell had happened?! He felt hot and feverish in the small room with high humidity.

Mental pictures appeared before Brinker's eyes. He saw the radio equipment destroyed, Abert with his bleeding arm positioned in front of the SS men with their guns aimed at him. He remembered opening the turret hatch. He recalled the terrible confrontation with the SS officers, the explosion in the bow room. He saw the bodies of the SS men and then Krantz's body falling overboard. He remembered the helmsman looking at him with a horrified face, trembling and collapsing. He realized with horror that his submarine was lost. The terrible weapon still aboard the sub. How can I get in touch with Americans in Cuba? Am I already in their hands? Saved by a group of young women? What do I have to keep secret from the enemy? He decided to continue to play the game of suffering from amnesia.

The door opened and a blond woman walked to his bedside. "How are you?" she asked. "Do you understand me?"

No answer. Only a helpless look at her.

"Are you Dutch? From Jamaica?" the woman asked. "I'm Michele Bradburry. My friends found you floating in the ocean."

The friendly woman explained to him how the four women had hauled him aboard their yacht.

He heard himself asking the third watch officer after a sweep with the periscope, "Have you seen that white sail ahead of us?"

The woman was taking hold of him. She told him he was saved from the ocean where he drifted in a black rubber boat.

He was now in Cuba in the summer home of a young American woman. A doctor would be coming to see him within the next hour. "Do you understand me?" she asked.

A weak smile and nodding was the answer.

Then Michele gave him the world news. The war in Europe was coming to an end, Germany expected to surrender at any moment. Hitler was dead, Berlin in Russian hands, Göring arrested, Himmler disappeared and Admiral Dönitz the new leader.

Five days later Michele was caring for Brinker as if he were her brother. He said he still suffered from steady headaches which, fortunately, were losing some of their intensity. She told him about her life in Cuba as an American citizen. When she described her job as secretary at the American base at Guantánamo Bay, she felt him stiffen and close up.

She kept asking him where he came from, but always got the same answer, "Sorry. I don't recall." He could only remember his first name — Hans. When asked how he got to the region where he was picked up, it was the same words: "I don't recall anything. Please, have patience with me. I must get my memory back."

Dr. Kruse, a family doctor from the Cuban countryside, found that the patient had probably suffered from some poisoning, but could not get any specifics. He called by phone every day and got the same report from Michele that the stranger was improving but his memory had gone.

"Should I call the police to help you?" the doctor asked. "They'll take him to a hospital where he won't take up your time."

"Oh no," she answered quickly. "Please don't alert anybody. I don't want crowds of people around my house. It would embarrass me tremendously. I know he will improve soon."

Michele didn't want to lose the stranger. She wanted to care for this man who couldn't remember anything. Isn't it awful not knowing what had happened in the past? she pondered. She enjoyed watching his face relax when she told him of news she'd heard on the radio. She showed him the newspaper which didn't mean anything to him because he couldn't read Spanish. But his understanding of English seemed to improve day by day.

"This day the war in Europe ended," Michele told him. "The German military surrendered to the Allied forces. At noon shooting stopped."

"Really?" he asked. "The war is over?" His face shone.

Michele continued translating from the paper: "General Jodl and Admiral Frydeburg have signed the surrender."

He jumped up from his bed and asked to see the paper. "*Nein*, Friedeburg is his name," he said, pronouncing it like Freedeboorg. He pointed to the name. "Now I'm free. Now I can answer your questions!"

From this moment he was another person. He told Michele he was the *Kommandant* of a German U-boat that had sunk shortly before he was picked up. He was the sole survivor. He had felt bound to his oath not to reveal any secrets to the enemy. Now with the war over and his former admiral of the U-boat service having signed the surrender, he wanted to get in touch with an American naval officer as quickly as possible. "You said you worked for the naval base. I'm sorry, I had to be silent so you wouldn't turn me in. Can you phone the base? I have top secret information which I wish to hand over."

Michele, wondering about the sudden turn of events, called her boss. When she hung up, she told him, "Admiral Curtis is sending two captains to see you."

35. Guantánamo Bay, Cuba - May 10, 1945.

Erik Svensen arrived by plane from Washington, D.C. and spoke for two hours with Hans Brinker. Erik heard with surprise what had happened on U-888 and decided to keep the existence of the special mission of the U-boat and its secret weapon to himself. And the *Kommandant* was amazed how much the OSS knew about his boat and the secrecy kept by the Americans.

"I assumed you wouldn't know anything about our patrol," Brinker said. "For that reason I revealed nothing to Admiral Curtis and his officers. I only demanded to be put in contact with the highest U.S. Naval Intelligence authority. We must take steps to eliminate the threat of the miracle weapon, salvage the boat and destroy the missiles."

"The plans will be worked out in Washington,D.C.," Erik said. "My plane is waiting for us on the tarmac."

36. Havana, Cuba - May 14, 1945.

A tavern in downtown Havana, run by a German immigrant, catered to Germans and their friends who wanted to drink a good beer in this tropical city. A group of nine SS men who worked in Havana during the war as spies for Himmler's Security Service met with their boss in the tavern. The boss was known as Heinz. His family name, Berger, was never used. Nobody knew if this was his real name or not. On letters, telegrams and other secret reports his name was MONTBLANC. Heinz brought a guest to the meeting, a man who seemed to be very taciturn to the SS men. The last person to arrive was a woman friend of Heinz, known to be always late.

He organized the group in the late 1930s when their task was to keep a sharp eye on Germans who had left Germany, mostly dissidents or Jews. After the Japanese attacked Pearl Harbor, this focus had changed. Hitler declared war against the United States and a few weeks later the first German submarines appeared a few miles off the U.S. East Coast sinking tankers. MONTBLANC and his men worked as spies reporting through Spain about American activities in Cuba. Soon this field widened when German subs also sailed into the Carribean Sea and sank countless ships.

The mood of the men was miserable. The war was lost, ending in a complete surrender, Hitler, Himmler and all German party leaders reported dead or arrested. There was no purpose any longer for the intelligence group that worked for Himmler. The men discussed the possibility of being arrested by the Cuban government. Or maybe by the American government. They were sure American intelligence knew about them and their activities. The men talked about breaking up and looking for new jobs where they could go into hiding.

"We must tint our blond hair black, grow beards and disappear into the countryside," Walter, MONTBLANC's assistant, said.

"I think we should even leave Cuba. Why don't we go to

Argentina?" a tall man named Ernesto said. "We still have enough money for ship tickets."

"*Verdammte Sauerei!* — Dammed pig shit! Now I've heard enough!" the guest yelled, banging his fist on the table. "You've been SS men who swore eternal fidelity to Hitler and Himmler, the representatives of our Greater Germany! Where is your loyalty to our Aryan *Reich*?"

The guest turned to Heinz. "Present me to your men and tell them how I came here to meet them."

Heinz took a deep breath. "You'll be surprised to see *Standartenführer* Krantz among you. He was under special order from our *Reichsführer* to deploy the Miracle Weapon against America. Treason of the *Kriegsmarine* delayed this and hindered him from bringing the Final Victory to our nation. Through help of Divine Providence, he was found by fishermen on the high seas and brought back to shore where he found his way to our office. Now he is here and expects you to be his followers to create a New Germany." Heinz's voice rose with every word. "Stand up with me and greet him as our new *Führer*. *Heil* Krantz!"

"*Heil* Krantz!" yelled the eight men and the woman, jumping from their chairs and raising their right arms in salute.

Krantz began his speech. "Not everything is lost. If we continue fighting, we can turn around the fate of our nation. I'm one of Adolf Hitler's earliest trusted followers. I worked with the Superior SS Staff directly under our *Reichsführer*. I've read your reports in my Berlin office. You've done an excellent job. Now listen to me! I still have my hands on a weapon that can turn everything to our advantage."

He now employed a method used by Hitler when he bluffed European politicians by lying and distorting facts leading to a political victory.

Mesmerized, the SS men looked at their guest who continued speaking to them.

"When I use this weapon, it will kill twenty to thirty million Americans. Truman and Churchill will be forced to come to an agreement with me to re-arm the *Waffen SS* troops. We and the Americans will then march against Stalin together. Victory over the Siberian communist hordes will give us our New Greater Germany. That is my goal. It should also be yours. If we hold together we'll create a *Reich* that spreads from the Rhine River to the Ural mountains. We can rule Europe, and the Americans and British will rule the *natives* in the colonies."

The men and one woman listened for the next two hours to the plan of their energetic new *Führer*.

37. Washington, D.C. - May 18, 1945.

Senior analyst Russ Bender was busy in his office in the OSS building in Washington when Armando Cuevas, Abe Weinstein's expert on Cuba, reported and made a proposal to eliminate a group of SS officers who worked in Cuba during the war. "These guys worked in Matanzas directly under Himmler's orders. Maybe they had information about the weapon. We should get missing data from their chief Heinz Berger."

"Not bad, Armando," Russ said. "Would you take the assignment?"

"I feel that as a former Cuban citizen I wouldn't have the necessary authority and connections to the Embassy and Naval Institutions for this job. Wouldn't Erik have more success in working with those offices? It means the arrest of foreigners in Cuba with the agreement of the Cuban government."

"Maybe you are right. I'll speak to Erik and make flight arrangements to Cuba."

38. Havana, Cuba - May 24, 1945.

"What's the rank of that Norwegian fellow? What's his name?" Krantz asked.

"Svensen. He's the man assigned to U-888 and the miracle weapon. Most dangerous, Pluto told me," Heinz said.

"Then we must shoot him!" Krantz suggested.

"Too dangerous," Heinz's girlfriend Ariana said. "You'll be caught by the Cuban police. All your plans will be stopped. It'll take a long time until my friends can get you out of jail. It will require much money to bribe the police."

"But he must be liquidated. I can't use that pig as Truman's informer!" Krantz said. "This man knows too much!"

"We'll work it out," Heinz said.

146

39. Havana, Cuba - May 26, 1945.

In Havana Erik was not optimistic. It had been a busy, tiring, unsuccessful day. Nothing had worked. All his leads on the SS men were negative. Berger's house in Matanzas, under surveillance, remained empty. Berger and his "cousins" had disappeared.

Frustrated, Erik went into the hotel bar and ordered a bourbon on the rocks. A pianist played soft Latin American music while a dark-skinned girl sang in a seductive voice. Exotic flowers spread a sweet fragrance through the room.

A woman took an empty seat at the other end of the bar and ordered a *mojito*, a rum mint julep, the Cuban national drink. She talked with the bartender and spoke about the end of the war and what it could mean to Cuba.

God, she was beautiful! Erik thought. Blond hair fell over lightly tanned shoulders. Fragile straps held up an elegant purple and green dress that did nothing to conceal the size and shape of her full breasts. She played with the hem of a long, turquoise silk shawl draped around her shoulders. No woman would ever wear such exotic colors in England or the United States.

Erik, attracted, picked up his drink and sat beside her. "I should've ordered a *mojito* too."

Her smile was brilliant, her lips moist. "I love *mojitos*."

He liked her low, intimate voice. "Are you Swedish?" he asked. "Your accent sounds familiar."

"No. German. But I live here."

Surprised at his good luck, he ordered a drink for himself and the woman.

"Have you had difficulties in this country being a German?" he asked.

"Not at all. There is no animosity toward Germans. My husband was very active in the German *Verein* before his death."

"I'm sorry. Is the club part of the German government?"

"No. It's an organization that unites Germans living in foreign countries. However, the new immigrants and the dissidents don't join, so it isn't as powerful as it should be. Are you in Havana on vacation?"

"On a short business trip," he said. "Let me introduce myself. Olaf Torgersen."

"My name is Lulu, Lulu Steinburg." She extended her hand. Her flesh was warm and firm, her grip easy. When Erik held onto her hand longer than necessary, she smiled and withdrew it.

"My husband was busy most of the time. He was always visiting other members of the German club. I didn't see too much of him, except when we spent time together at our summer house in Matanzas."

Warning signals ran down Erik's back. A German woman from Matanzas on the bar stool beside him? What a coincidence! "I once had a friend whose address I lost during the war," he said. "My friend lived in Matanzas."

"Maybe I know him. Was he Norwegian?"

"Berger was his name... "

"Of course, Heini Berger," Lulu said with a friendly smile. "He lives in Havana now. He also belongs to the *Verein*."

She took his hand and held it. Her eyes sparkled. "What a surprise. We have mutual friends."

His hand tingled from her touch. What the hell! It had been a long time since a beautiful woman held his hand. "Bartender," he ordered. "Two glasses of champagne." Turning to her he said, "We must celebrate."

She smiled again. "How long is this short business trip of yours?"

"I'm leaving tomorrow."

She sighed. "So soon?"

The champagne cork exploded and the bartender filled two glasses. Erik raised his glass. "To the most beautiful woman in Cuba."

Lulu's eyes met his over the rim of her glass. "To our

friendship," Lulu replied, looking deep into his eyes. She put her glass down and leaned against his arm. Her perfume was light but compelling.

"Olaf, I find you very attractive," she whispered. "I hope I'm not being too forward, but having mutual friends like this and our both being European ... well, I thought we might mark this day. It's terrible for a woman to be alone." She kissed him softly on the side of his mouth, her lips demanding. He turned his head quickly and kissed her full on her soft lips. He drew back, startled at his own response to her. Her open face offered compassion, sensuality and yes, even eagerness.

Stroking her arm, he breathed in her ear, "How long have you known Heinz Berger?"

"For many years. I have his address upstairs, if you want it," she spoke meaningfully. He smiled, his hand covered hers. They both emptied their glasses and stood up.

The hotel elevator was empty. When the door closed, Lulu turned to Erik and pressed her body against his. He held her face in his hands and kissed her gently. It had been a long time since he'd held a woman like this. He hungered for her, but he didn't want to move too quickly. The elevator stopped at the sixth floor. She took a large key from her purse as they moved down the long hall to the last door, Room 622.

"Excuse the mess," she said, her voice low. "I'm afraid the maid hasn't been here to clean up."

He quickly scanned the room, one of the most expensive in the hotel. Large windows on both sides of the huge bed faced the door. A bathroom was on the far side. The bed was unmade, and dresses, panties, bras and nylons had been tossed over an armchair and some dropped on the floor. Close to the door sat a small refrigerator beside a chest of drawers.

She threw her handbag and shawl on the chair and walked to the chest of drawers and lit four candles. She left two on the chest and put two on a nightstand, then picked up a bowl and spread something around the room that already seemed to be filled with the smell of lust. It was the same aroma he'd smelled in the bar when he sat next to her. As he was thinking he would never forget her perfume the lights were turned off and she opened the window. He moved behind her, his hands on her shoulders. She pulled them down to her breasts and held them there. The warm subtropical air blew into the room. A band played *La cucaracha, la cucaracha*, the sound pulsating up from six floors below. They swayed their bodies in time to the Latin rhythm.

"Isn't it beautiful?" she whispered.

"You're beautiful."

She leaned back against his body. "Undress me," she said in a low voice.

He undid the buttons on the back of her dress and pulled it down, sliding the straps over her arms. From behind he embraced her, cupping her full breasts with his hands.

She turned, standing before him, her large, dark-brown nipples erect.

He would ask for Berger's address later.

Smiling, she looked in his eyes and removed his tie, unbuttoned his shirt, pulled it off and dropped it to the floor. She lay her head on his chest and wrapped her arms around him. Her warm, smooth flesh against his bare chest sent his heart racing. He kissed her and drove his tongue deep inside her mouth.

He pulled her dress down over her hips. She stepped out of it, then kicked her shoes into the corner of the room. He unhooked her delicate, transparent stockings from her garter belt and knelt down to peel them from her legs. A small French triangle of lace barely covered the dark hair in her crotch, a contrast to the blond hair on her head. Well, so what? A genuine blonde wasn't that important, he thought, as he pulled the lace triangle down, baring the tight, curly hair and kissed the hidden wet lips. She had sprayed perfume between her legs and, dizzy with his mounting desire, he held her with his mouth. Then he rose to his feet and kissed her breasts.

With experienced hands she unbuttoned his fly and pulled his pants and briefs down. "My God!" she whispered. Her fingers closed over his hardness and massaged him. "I didn't expect such an athlete!" she marveled. "A Viking for a hungry woman! I can hardly wait!"

He pulled her body tightly to his. Naked, they stood beside the bed, swaying. His hands were all over her body and played with the hardening nub between her legs. He turned her around so her back was to him and pushed his body against her buttocks. He used one hand to play with her breasts, circling his fingers around her firm nipples. When he heard a soft moaning, he lowered her to the bed on her knees and elbows and took her from behind, penetrating her slowly.

He kept firm contact, his body over hers, holding her breasts with both hands. She turned her head and looked roguishly at him. He felt her body quiver as she moaned, "Yes — yes — Yes!" Her groans grew to a triumphant shout of joy. He thrust repeatedly into her and the brilliant flash of a sexual thunderstorm shook both their bodies in a tremor of lust.

Breathing heavily, they collapsed on the bed, their arms around each other.

They relaxed side by side as she stroked the hair on his chest and fondled his member. When it was hard again, he turned on his back and motioned for her to sit on top of him. She moved above him, her breasts swinging, her rhythmic motions building his desire when their bodies were united. As he felt her shudder, he forced her back down on the bed and moved on top of her, his erect shaft between her breasts, which she softly pressed together with her hands. He brought himself to a frenzy. A line of silvery sperm droplets rushed down both sides of her neck like a moving pearl necklace.

She twisted and moaned, lost in the waning ecstasy of her own orgasm.

He rolled off her. She lifted herself up on her elbows. "Take a rest, darling," she said, her voice unexpectedly calm. "I'll fix us a drink."

She got up, put on a white robe and stepped over to the small refrigerator beside the door.

Still breathing heavily, he watched as she took two glasses from a shelf and a rum bottle from the refrigerator. She picked up a full glass jar from the floor and put it next to the rum bottle.

Before he understood what she was doing, he saw her topple the glass jar. There was the sound of breaking glass. "Hey!" he yelled. Was she crazy? It was the smell of gasoline that brought him to his feet. "Look out!"

Before he could reach her, she swept the two candles from the chest of drawers onto the spilled gasoline. It ignited with a whoosh, creating a barrier of red, yellow and blue flames between them.

Unchecked, the fire flashed across the floor, spreading to the furniture and the bed. He grabbed his pants and realized she had run out of the room and closed the door behind her. He heard the clicking noise of a key.

Can I escape through the window? he wondered frantically. He ran to look out — six floors down.

His only way out was through the door! He pulled his pants on, wrestled the mattress off the bed and onto the flames. He ran on top of the mattress to the locked door.

He shook the door handle. It was locked tight. He banged on the wood panels. The heat and smoke became unbearable. He grabbed a chair, ramming it against the door. Fortunately, the chair was solid. The door began to break. Another hit. And another. He coughed — the room was full of smoke and flames. The door broke and he squeezed himself through the opening into the hall.

Erik gasped for air, his smoke-filled lungs burning with the effort. "Use the stairs," he mumbled. "When there's a fire, use the stairs."

At the end of the long hallway he saw Lulu jump into the elevator. He ran toward it.

The elevator was gone. He ran down the stairs. Reaching the ground floor, he looked for Lulu. He saw her out on the street, getting into a car that disappeared with screeching tires.

He ran toward the hotel counter. "Fire! Fire on the sixth floor!" he cried hoarsely.

The man behind the desk pushed a shiny bronze button on the wall. An alarm sounded immediately.

"Fire! Fire! Leave the hotel!" the receptionist yelled at the startled hotel guests in the lobby.

Erik, still fighting to breathe, watched the procession of women in nightgowns, men in pajamas, and half-dressed children rush down the staircases, yelling and crying.

"*¡Madre de Dios*! Help! Help! Police!"

At every moment the tumult grew louder.

Erik could now feel the agony on his feet, legs and back. He was burned. His pants were scorched at the cuff and small holes like cigarette burns dotted the fabric.

Lulu Steinburg had meant to burn him to death! Why?

40. Jibacoa, Cuba - May 30, 1945.

"I did it, Albert!" Ariana shouted when Krantz entered the house. "He's dead! He'll never bother you any more."

"Really? Are you sure? Give me a drink, quick!"

"Didn't you read the papers? *Ach*, you can't read Spanish."

"I was busy with my men in the center."

"That American pig! He couldn't keep his hands off my body and his fingers touched me everywhere. Well, I set him on fire. He's fucking in hell now!" She laughed with a bone-shattering coolness. "I told him my name was Lulu."

"I'm thirsty. Damned! Bring me a beer, quick."

Ariana went to the refrigerator. She poured beer into a beerstein and handed it to him.

After drinking half of the stein in one single gulp, he said: "This climate is hell! So hot, so muggy!"

"There has been mention of six charred bodies," Ariana said, continuing the conversation she started.

"How do you know he's one of them?" Krantz asked coldly.

"I locked him in, darling Albert. There is no way he could get out. Believe me, he's dead."

"I hope so. He worried me."

She leaned over and kissed the top of his head. "It has been almost four days. I want to celebrate. Must I beg you to come to bed with me?"

She slid to the floor and wrapped her arms around his legs, her eyes bright, her mouth moist and open. "Shall we do it here? On the rug?"

"You're an animal, Ariana."

She smiled and caressed the front of his pants. "Pretty please, Albert."

As always in their lovemaking, she was the aggressor, his cold indifference spurring her on to ever more erotic behavior. He couldn't resist. Soon they were naked and rolling on the rug.

Later she walked through the house naked and brought him

154

another beer.

"You see, Albert, the danger is over. The American is no longer a threat. No one can prove you killed the submarine crew and your people. You're free to return to Germany and begin your plans for the future. We can take an Italian liner to Europe. From there we'll travel to Germany. I'll pay for the trip. It's time to start the new Germany."

Theirs was a strange relationship. After the meeting eight days ago in the beer cellar, she had invited him to live in her luxurious summer home in Jibacoa. When he explained his plan to kill the American agent, she feared he'd be arrested and put into a Cuban jail. That would keep him from realizing his plans for months, if not years, until she could use bribes and the influence of her friends to have him released.

Convinced that going to jail would endanger his political future, he agreed to let *her* do the job of killing Erik Svensen.

The illegitimate child of a rich German industrialist and a French movie actress, Ariana had been sent to Cuba when she was eighteen years old. Her father provided her with enough money to live in the high society of the subtropical island. Men were a necessity for her, but she never found one she could trust enough to marry. She knew they loved her money more than they did her, so she detested and used them. During the last twenty years she thought only of her own pleasure and changed lovers so often her affairs were the hottest gossip of Havana. She lived a life of lust and debauchery with a group of old and new friends in one of the most elegant beach homes in Jibacoa, a beautiful resort a hundred miles east of Havana.

Now she had met a man she could admire: Albert Krantz. He was the first man who neglected her completely. He wasn't even polite. He didn't get up from his lounge chair when she entered the room. He never kissed her hand; he never bowed. He just didn't take any notice of her, except when he wanted a drink. She found his arrogance intriguing and was proud that she could assist him and his SS corps.

She longed to be the wife of a world leader and was

determined to use her money and rich friends of her family in Germany to finance Krantz's rise to power. She and Krantz must travel to Europe as soon as possible.

She made a few telephone calls and found an Italian ocean liner would be the first ship to sail from Havana to Genoa after the war ended. She ordered two tickets and prepared everything for the trip, asking one of her friends to take care of the house during her absence.

The next day Ariana Herzog and Albert Krantz drove to Havana and one day later they were on the RICARDO BENVENUTO.

Standing with him on deck, Ariana felt as though she were beginning a new life. Ahead of her stretched a magnificent future with her man by her side, his plans for the world financed with her money. She had never felt like this before. She slipped her hand under his coat and inside his pants.

"Let's go to our cabin, darling. I have something for the new *Führer*."

To her surprise, she felt him harden. It never happened that fast before. Pleased that she had discovered something new about her lover, she continued to call him the "new *Führer*" as she hurried him to their stateroom.

41. Havana, Cuba - June 5, 1945.

Lieutenant John Hazelton, a young assistant to Erik from the U.S.Embassy, lounged by the pool of the "Hotel Caribia." Known in Havana as a playboy, as usual he had two beautiful girls with him. Elena, slim and flat-bodied, and Marina, in a swimsuit that emphasized her high, pointed breasts. Elena left to greet friends arriving at the pool.

Marina asked John, "When can we go on vacation again?

"How about a week in Jamaica?"

"No, I've already been there."

"Barbados?"

"I had a bad time with Carlos. *Nunca más*! Never again."

"Who is Carlos? Do I know him?"

"I think you're jealous," she teased. "Don't worry about Carlos. He's a bastard and deserves the German woman."

"What German woman?" John asked.

"Ariana. She has a home in Jibacoa and hangs around with Enrique's crowd from Matanzas. I see her occasionally in Havana. You must know her."

John's thoughts raced. He knew she was talking about the leader of the German spy organization. He asked: "What does she look like?"

Marina seemed surprised. "I suppose you men know her. You would call her gorgeous, but she bleaches her hair and she's forty if she's a day."

"And her name?"

"Ariana Herzog. How's that for a mouthful?"

"And she knows Enrique?" John asked, using the Spanish name for Heinz.

"Intimately, I would say. That's the way she knows all men." Marina giggled. "That is, until the last one. He's a brutal wolf, if you ask me."

"Who? Carlos?"

"No, no. Not Carlos. He was last month. Alberto. I mean the

Nazi Ariana is dragging around now."

"How do you know he's a Nazi?"

Elena came back and sat down beside Sylvia.

"She fired her Negro butler at the German's request," Marina answered. "He said he didn't want to stay in a house with a Negro. And he doesn't speak Spanish. Can you imagine, people say he was fished from the ocean!"

John was thrilled. His thoughts tumbled over themselves, one after the other. "Does this man now live in Jibacoa?"

Marina shook her head. "They took a ship to Italy. Three days ago. Isn't that right, Elena?"

"It was in the paper," Elena agreed. "Ariana sailed to Genoa on the RICARDO BENVENUTO."

John looked at his watch. "I have to go. I'm late already. *Con permiso*. Maybe I'll see you here tomorrow."

He made a phone call, then drove to his office where he waited impatiently for Erik to arrive. It was seven days since the hotel fire and Erik still limped on sore feet.

"Erik, is it possible that Krantz lives? I heard a fantastic story!" John said and reported his conversation with Marina and Elena.

"You mean Krantz could be picked up like Brinker?" Erik asked. "That's impossible! I can't believe that."

"Why not? His name is Albert, he's called a Nazi and was fished from the ocean. Everything points to it being Albert Krantz."

"And he went to Italy?"

"Look on the bright side," John said cheerfully. "Three days ago you could barely walk. Now at least you can go after him."

They drove to the harbor. Isidoro Benavides, the harbor master, informed Erik and John that the RICARDO BENVENUTO had indeed sailed for Genoa three days ago.

"Let's go to Ernesto and see his photos," John suggested.

As always when an ocean liner left port, Ernesto Ritter took photos of the people on deck before the ship left the pier. He was a professional photographer who shot the pictures with his

Leica, developed them, and put them on sale for friends or family members staying in Havana. It made a nice extra income.

John led Erik to Ritter's studio where the photographer had a window filled with his latest photos.

"Could this be Ariana?" John asked, pointing to a blond woman next to a tall haughty man.

"Ah, Lulu! Yes!" Erik exclaimed. "We'll meet again. I've a score to settle with you."

"She's the one?" John asked. "You mean my Marina has helped to find your Lulu?"

Erik nodded. "Be sure to give Marina my love. I owe her one. And this man next to her must be Krantz." Erik bought the picture from Ritter.

They returned to the harbor master to ask when the BENVENUTO was scheduled to arrive in Genoa.

"In ten days, on June 15."

Good, Erik thought. More than enough time to fly there and give them a grand reception.

42. OSS Office, Washington, D.C. - June 7, 1945.

Erik was thoroughly familiar with the way from the airport to OSS headquarters on the Potomac River, and could sit back and enjoy the drive.

His first stop was at his boss's ultra-modern office. He thought of the many hours he spent there, analyzing with Russ Bender what might be the next move of the supersecret U-boat. He liked Russ Bender. They worked well together.

"Back again from the tropics? Aren't you freezing here?" Russ asked cordially.

"Imagine, Krantz is alive!" Erik interrupted his greeting. "I've a picture of him and his Cuban supporter. Brinker must look at this photo and confirm Krantz's existence!" Then he reported the happenings in Cuba.

Russ was shocked. "Brinker is the only one who knows Krantz. I'll call him."

"What is the progress of the salvage of our U-boat? Has Brinker been helpful?"

"Without him it would be impossible to go ahead. He's a real pusher, an unbelievably energetic officer. I can understand why he was such a successful U-boat commander."

Bender offered Erik a cup of coffee. "If Hans — we call Brinker now by his first name — recognizes Krantz, you'll have to fly to Italy," he said.

"I'll get him in Genoa for sure. He'll find an unexpected reception at the pier. He's an extremely dangerous man. We must catch him."

"I hope so. Good luck, Erik!"

43. Genoa, Italy - June 15, 1945.

Genoa is the largest port on Northern Italy's west coast. Christopher Columbus was born here and sailed from this port to offer his services to the kings of Portugal and Spain.

It was in Genoa that Erik arrived on a military plane to organize the arrest of Krantz. After his arrival, Erik immediately contacted the general of the American forces and arranged for a lieutenant who spoke Italian as well as English. He also asked for a group of soldiers to watch the pier and the surrounding area for the SS man and Ariana Herzog. The Italian harbor master was contacted just an hour before three tugboats pushed the BENVENUTO to the pier. Soldiers lined the gangplank to keep the crowd away while Erik and the lieutenant stepped aboard, followed by the Italian customs officers and six American sergeants with concealed weapons.

The BENVENUTO's captain gave instructions over the intercom for each passenger to wait in his cabin with his custom forms filled out until the customs officer could go through the ship.

Erik learned from the purser that Ariana Herzog and her husband occupied Stateroom No. 12 on the top deck, one of the most expensive rooms. The purser accompanied Erik and the six armed petty officers to room No. 12. Except for three heavy pieces of luggage on the bed, the room was empty.

The purser picked up the telephone and called the captain. The intercom once again carried the captain's voice with instructions for all passengers to report to their cabins, but Erik and his group waited in vain.

The couple in the stateroom next door were asked about the Herzogs. They reported seeing their neighbors leave the ship in the motorboat of the quarantine doctor outside the three-mile limit.

The lieutenant asked other passengers if they had seen the Herzogs. They confirmed they'd seen a tall man and blond woman leave the ship early. There had been some speculation as to whether or not the blond woman and her husband were under quarantine. It was hoped they had nothing contagious.

A waitress said: "They took all their meals in their room, never went to the dining room. Very strange people."

Undaunted, Erik went to the bridge to see the captain. "Is it normal for people to leave your ship with the quarantine doctor?"

"No, sir. This couple may have somehow persuaded the doctor to let them go. That is entirely possible."

"Did you see them leaving?"

"Yes, sir. But it was too late to interfere."

The first officer grinned. "They probably had money. Doctors have to make a living too."

Frustrated, Erik didn't answer.

Krantz and Lulu had slipped through his fingers! Where was he going to find them in the chaos of a destroyed Europe? He gave orders to have the luggage, left in Stateroom 12, sent to American headquarters. He searched the stateroom himself, but found nothing except a calendar from which the address pages were ripped off.

44. Bern, Switzerland - June 22, 1945.

After arriving in Genoa on the quarantine doctor's boat, Krantz was surprised to see how well Ariana took the initiative to hide them from Allied authorities in Italy. She contacted a representative of the Vatican right away. To win him over she made a large contribution to the religious Institute Santa Maria dell Anima in Rome. She knew the Vatican supported Nazi Germany during the war and continued to support persecuted Nazis as allies against the communists. So she asked the monsignor to help them get to Switzerland. The priest immediately understood. He allowed them to hide in a nun's cloister where they would be safe from Nazi hunters. Krantz was introduced to the Mother Superior as a plumber, there to repair rotten, rusty pipes. Ariana was dressed in a nun's cowl and pretended to participate in the daily prayers. Staff members of a bishop in Rome provided them with false Red Cross passports, entry visas, and train tickets to Bern. After a few days they left for Switzerland.

Krantz wanted to begin his political struggle in Switzerland, where Ariana found shelter for the two of them in the villa of one of her father's friends.

Remembering the intelligence center in the Herrengasse in Bern, Krantz visited it and met several of his friends. He invited himself to a meeting of a dozen SS officers who met to make plans for the future. The group gathered on the third floor in a bare room with only a long table and chairs. Most men present were fugitives, their civilian clothes bizarre combinations of cast-off garments scrounged during their escapes. The leader was Herbert Gockel, standing at the head of the table, dressed in brown breeches, an orange-beige shirt and a green jacket so small his sleeves stopped below his elbows.

By contrast Krantz wore a well-tailored suit, which Ariana bought for him when they reached Bern. As Krantz entered the room, Gockel was speaking.

" ...destination. Our continuous acts of sabotage will force the Allied troops to leave Germany," he explained to the silent SS officers. "I'll be your leader in organizing the destruction of still functioning bridges, port facilities and locomotives."

Karl Stumpf, an elderly SS colonel from Himmler's former staff, countered: "Not enough. The enemy will stay."

"We'll wear them down," Gockel continued. "If not, we'll destroy churches and the food storage buildings."

Krantz strongly disagreed with Gockel's plans, but kept silent. He let the group continue the discussion. The men could agree on nothing and shortly before lunch, Krantz's patience was exhausted. He got up, banged his fist on the table and looked at each member of the group.

"Enough!" he shouted. "You can't find any German who will destroy food. They've nothing to eat any more. Your plans are negative and must fail. Only a positive plan will have success."

Startled, the SS officers stiffened in their chairs.

SS Colonel Stumpf asked: "What kind of positive plan?"

"I'll tell you. We have to work *with* the Western Allies, not against them. We'll offer to fight with them against the commies. With their help we'll mobilize all SS troops and re-arm them. Only with support from the Western armies can we build a new *Reich*."

Gockel snorted. "Himmler tried this plan," he said with bitterness. "Eisenhower and Montgomery rejected it. I listened to the phone conversation between Himmler and Count Bernadotte myself. The *Reichsführer* made the same proposal. You'll fail as Himmler did. The Western generals are tired of fighting."

"Himmler had no leverage," Krantz countered. "I'm in a different position. I'm in charge of the unused Miracle Weapon and will use it as blackmail. I can kill thirty million people if Truman and Churchill don't accept my plan."

With short staccato sentences he explained the status of the miracle weapon, still unused on board U-888. He lied, distorting details to produce a more favorable picture of the actual situation, as well as omitting the fact that he even didn't know the position of the U-boat.

"I can activate the weapon any time I wish," he fibbed. "I'll use this to force the British and Americans to negotiate with me."

The officers, listening attentively, looked at Krantz with new hope.

At this moment, Ariana entered the room, wearing an elegant silk dress, her blond hair falling in smooth waves over the contrasting black collar. She carried a white shoulder bag and wore shoes that emphasized the perfect shape of her legs. Everyone turned to stare.

Krantz presented her to the surprised officers: "This is *Frau* Herzog. She has assisted our cause in Cuba in a selfless and extremely courageous manner. She joined our group and will work with us for a new German *Reich*. I want you to accept *Frau* Herzog as a member of our corps."

He got an extra chair from the corner of the room, putting it at his side. The men, who had risen to their feet, greeted her with the Nazi salute.

Gockel made an attempt to regain his place as leader. "Why did you never report from U-888 to the *Führer* headquarters?" he asked Krantz in a sharp voice. "Himmler waited in vain for your message that would bring us the Final Victory. Where is the U-boat? It looks like your mission failed completely."

Krantz flushed with rage. "*You* didn't provide sufficient diesel fuel for the U-boat! We reached Cuba after Hitler's death."

"Schmeltzer prepared the plan. Not me!" Gockel shouted.

"Hitler and Himmler are dead," Krantz continued, his rage gone in the face of Gockel's self-serving denial. "Your mistakes now help me to use the weapon for our cause. I can threaten Truman and Churchill. They know about U-888 and the weapon."

"How do they know?" Gockel demanded.

"Pluto, our man in Washington, reported to us in Havana and identified an American spy who came to Cuba to catch me. The sub was tracked from Norway to Cuba. The Americans have even guessed what the miracle weapon is. They think they are so smart, but I am always one step ahead of them. When I speak, they will listen."

"What's the name of the spy?" asked a tall, young SS officer, who worked in Bern for the last three years in counterespionage.

Ariana spoke up. "Erik Svensen," she said. "An American pig who burned to death in a hotel fire. Only his bones remain."

"That's not true!" the tall, young man declared. "He's recently been seen in Genoa."

"Nonsense," Ariana said with emphasis. "I should know. I killed him!"

"I can show you his picture," the young man said in a calm voice. "I have it in my safe on the fourth floor. I'll get it for you."

Krantz became angry about this disturbance. A minute later the man returned. There was a sudden silence as he showed Krantz and Ariana three photos.

Ariana recognized Erik Svensen. She was gasping and covering her mouth with her hand.

"When and where were these photos taken?" Krantz demanded.

"Six days ago in Genoa before he boarded the RICARDO BENVENUTO. Our man in Genoa took the pictures," the counterespionage officer said. "I received them this morning with a warning to watch out for him. This man has a lot of support from the American army."

Shocked, Krantz and Ariana stared at each other.

"Divine Providence has saved us," Krantz said with a mocking smile, using Hitler's favorite expression.

"No, not Providence," Ariana said. "*You* saved us. It was *your* idea to leave the ship with the quarantine doctor."

"I wonder how Svensen escaped from the burning hotel room," Krantz said. "I can assure you he won't be so lucky next time."

Krantz continued for the next two hours to explain his political plan for the future. He envisioned a new military struggle, victory over the communists, a triumphal march through Moscow and a Great Germany, stretching its influence from the Atlantic to the Urals. He could see the other officers were impressed. They could finally visualize a new future for their defeated country.

"We have to find Svensen and eliminate him," Krantz said at the end of his long talk. He turned to the young man with the pictures. "What do your sources say about Svensen? What's he doing now?"

"I got the pictures and the warning. Nothing else."

Krantz nodded. "Of course he will follow the trail of U-888, which means he could go to Wilhelmshaven or Berlin. Gockel, you will travel to the naval base in Wilhelmshaven. Search for him there and if you find him, kill him. Understand?"

Gockel hesitated, as though he might not accept the assignment, but when the other men in the room refused to meet his glance, he nodded. "Yes, sir."

"I myself will go to Berlin with *Frau* Herzog," Krantz said. "In case Svensen goes there first, we'll make sure he's killed. We've a lot of work to do to launch the new Great Germany. I cannot allow anyone to stand in my way."

Turning to the young officer he added: "Give me Svensen's pictures."

"Yes, sir."

He said to the group, "I expect you to prepare a schedule to re-arm and re-organize the SS divisions for our future war against the communists. Stumpf, you'll be responsible and must have the plan finished in two weeks. *Heil* Hit — ." He swallowed the last syllable of the dead *Führer*'s name and left the room. Ariana Herzog followed.

Walking together to their villa, Krantz angrily asked Ariana: "How do you explain Svensen's escape?"

"I don't know," she said, bewildered. "After the gasoline jar broke, the room was full of flames and smoke. He couldn't have left through the door. I locked it from the outside and left the key in the lock. He could only go through the window."

"On the sixth floor?"

"What else? It's the only explanation."

Krantz's glance was cold, his sneer disdainful. "When you begin to understand that there can be many explanations, then perhaps you'll carry out your assignments more carefully. I don't like Svensen's reappearance. It takes time away from my mission for the future. You saw those brave SS men today. They're with me. I can feel their dedication to me. We're on the threshold of a new era and what do *I* have to do? I'm forced to go to Berlin to deal with a spy I thought already dead. It's *your* fault, Ariana. You did not complete your assignment!"

They entered the villa in silence. In their room Krantz could control himself no longer. He hit her so hard she fell down. Then he kicked her and yelled: "Get your clothes off, damned woman!" He tore off his own clothing and cruelly punished her on the bed.

45. Washington, D.C. - June 23, 1945.

Russ Bender was outlining the different steps of the salvage operation when the door swung inward and Armando Cuevas, Abe Weinstein's staff specialist on Cuba, entered the room. He was a dark-haired man with a thin, attractive face and a wide smile. He explained that Abe had sent him to ask about the possible location of the U-boat along the Cuban coast.

"Abe doesn't want to alert the Cuban government, so he wishes to make our salvage as unsuspicious as possible." Cuevas said.

"If I'd know that," Russ said, "we would have started already. First we have to find the location."

"I don't like this German commander. Do we really need his assistance?"

"Sorry, I can't answer your question."

"I think he should be in jail as a war criminal. He definitely sank many ships and killed countless men of our navy. I'll do everything I can to make sure this guy gets what he deserves."

Russ ended the conversation by picking up his telephone and making a call.

Cuevas left the room. Russ wondered why this Cuban was so angry about Brinker. He was really part of the team working on the sub's salvage, very cooperative and well-liked. Every one called him Hans.

46. Washington, D.C. - June 25, 1945.

After receiving an interim report on the planned salvage of U-888, Abe felt satisfied. "Okay, you're on the right track," Abe told Russ. "We still have some loose ends. We don't know what happened to the SS spies in Cuba. Are they still there?"

"Maybe back in Germany like Krantz?" Russ said.

"I'm going to see if I can find out. It would answer a whole lot of questions if we could get these guys and make them talk. Armando Cuevas volunteered to go to Cuba himself and recruit the right people for the job. He's fluent in German, as well as in Spanish. He knows his country and is eager to get into the field after spending the war behind a desk. He'll work for you on land while you hunt for the sub."

Meetings between Russ, Erik and Hans continued over the next few weeks as their plans took shape and many details were worked out. The "Florida Towing and Salvage Company" was set up as a blind to cover their activities in Miami. They purchased two wooden fishing vessels, the HOPE and the ERNIE, and prepared them for the operation. Hans was of great help since he had all data about U-888 on hand. He had been concerned about the effects germs and gas could have on their effort to lift the submarine and asked Abe for support. Abe shared his anxiety and had taken steps to find help.

"We're faced with a red-hot sub if Krantz poisoned it. We'll have to treat it like it was radioactive." Abe looked at his watch. "I've asked one of Germany's best specialists to join us, gentlemen. He's an expert on germs and gas. He defected just before the war and came over to our side. I think you will find Dr. Bernstein a big asset. When and if you find the sub, he'll test the water for germs before the divers go down, and he'll test as much as he can to see if it's safe to enter. You must go slowly on every step of this search."

While they waited for Dr. Bernstein, they discussed the various

170

ways of raising the sub.

Finally, Abe sat back with a sigh. "It all comes down to the fact we don't know what you're going to find. My recommendation is to take all the equipment you think you'll need, as Hans proposed, pumps, compressors, something to add buoyancy — fishing balls or balloons — and decide what to do when you actually find the sub. There's even a chance you'll see the containers rolling around the bottom of the ocean and only bits and pieces of the sub. It's a crapshoot, gentlemen, and I wish to hell I could leave this desk and join you."

47. Berlin, British Sector - June 25, 1945.

Albert Krantz used every minute in total secrecy to begin his ascent as the new *Führer*. Each day he found SS men eager to struggle with him for a new Aryan Germany. The idea that had been created in the Havana beer cellar three months ago now grew in the harsh realities of post-war Germany. Krantz spoke every day to small groups of ten or fewer men, making them vow to keep their meetings secret. Fired up with the hope of coming to power again, each of them recruited other SS and former GESTAPO members. Krantz made sure to establish his role as leader. He used Hitler's methods of concentrating power in his own person, and of not tolerating any other individual's high visibility. He delegated tasks and ordered that the salute "Heil Krantz" be used exclusively during their meetings. He stressed that only strict obedience to his orders could guarantee success.

He steadily spoke about using the miracle weapon on U-888 to pressure Truman and Attlee to accept his plan of conquering the Soviet Union with joined forces and to re-establish a new Germany. Like Hitler, he spoke with such a self-trusting attitude that he convinced his followers of success. He stressed again and again that they must keep their activities completely secret. Their group soon grew to nine hundred fanatic followers and increased every day.

This rebirth of the SS gave the men hope for a future. Most German cities were destroyed; bridges, factories, schools and hospitals, all in ruins. Authority was gone. No government functioned any more, city councils and police powerless or in jail. All trains, busses and streetcars had stopped. There were no postal services, no radio, no newspapers. People who wanted to travel hiked from village to village during the night. The local officer of the occupation force was in charge of keeping law and order in the city or village in which he commanded his troops. Slowly, the Allied Military Government was trying to bring life back to the devastated country which had been plunged into chaos right after Germany's surrender. Most Nazis were in hiding under false names, trying to stay unrecognized, helping those in fear of being arrested. It was no wonder they felt relieved when they heard about Krantz's group. They saw their only salvation was in joining this group and supporting Krantz as the new *Führer*.

In the midst of his recruiting, Krantz received a note from the underground intelligence men who had received a message from MONTBLANC, their agent in Havana. Krantz must return to Cuba if he wanted his plan to succeed.

The sub! Krantz thought with rising excitement. They've found the sub! I must get it to blackmail Truman and Attlee.

He rushed to the room he shared with Ariana, shouting as he came through the door, "We must return to Cuba! Berger wants me there. Find us passage! The time has come!"

Ariana shared his jubilation. She complained constantly about living in the cold and destroyed Europe, saying she only wanted to return to Cuba's warm climate. Now she threw her arms around his neck and pressed her body tightly against his. Moments later they were together on the bed, their lovemaking wild and passionate.

48. Along the Cuban coast west of Isla de Piños - July 20, 1945.

The American salvage team, composed of Erik Svensen, *Kapitänleutnant* Hans Brinker and sixteen OSS men, had worked for two weeks and discovered the submarine after three day-and-night efforts along the Cuban coast. Hans was sure he had found a large metallic object that reflected the sound emitted from the search gear on board the HOPE. After Dr.Bernstein analyzed water samples, he suggested that two divers investigate the object.

Time crawled as Erik and the rest waited for some word from the divers. Finally, the younger one surfaced, two fingers spread in a "V" as he shouted, "We found it! We're now checking for damage." He disappeared underwater again.

When both divers surfaced, they climbed aboard excitedly. After pushing off his face mask, the younger man yelled, "It's unbelievable! The boat is completely intact. No damage at all. It's lying on its keel. Not the slightest sign of a malfunction. One periscope is raised and the turret hatch is open. All other hatches are closed."

"We found no bodies," the older diver said as he dropped his air tank to the deck. "There is no indication they got out or even tried to leave the sub. It's so perfect, it's like it was positioned there. It's kind of eerie."

By now the second salvage vessel, the ERNIE was alongside and Russ Bender, a celebration beer in hand, joined the discussion.

"The easiest way," Erik insisted, "would be to blow air into the sub's diving tanks to bring it to the surface. Am I right, Hans? We could send a hose down and pump air from the compressor in through the holes to the diving tank and raise it that way."

"Correct."

"If there's too much sandy floor in the way, we could also

174

pump water down and loosen the boat from the sand," Russ suggested.

"The sub will pop up too fast if we do it that way," Hans warned. "You'll have no control. We should do that only as a last resort."

"Maybe I'm stupid," Russ began, "but how about a sling under the thing and raise it that way?"

"Not enough power," Erik said, his mind busy. "Not even with both boats together."

"We have to control the buoyancy," Hans explained.

"We'll use the nets as Hans suggested," Erik decided. "How do we attach them, Hans?"

"Not to the wood grating on the deck. It would come loose. There are rows of holes in the outer hull parallel to the water line. You could put a rope in one hole and out the other. That way we attach the net to many holes, which should be a firm enough anchor. And we will use the glass balls for buoyancy."

"The boat was neutrally buoyant when it sailed at periscope depth," Erik said. "How much buoyancy do we need to compensate for the water in the upper turret room that was flooded?" he asked Hans.

"That's a very small room, only eight cubic meters. When the turret comes to the surface, we can pump out that water and let the conning tower stick out two or three feet."

"Right," Erik said. "Abe insisted we never show the whole contour of the U-boat to possible observers. We should tow the boat in this condition to Mexico."

After two days of hard work, taking glass balls down and under the net above the submarine, it rose until the turret deck surfaced. They pumped out the water in the periscope room, bringing the turret's pressure hull two feet above the water surface. They covered the turret with camouflage nets and towed the semi-submerged sub slowly southward, away from the Cuban coast. As soon as they were out of the Cuban three-mile zone, they changed course to the southwest.

At dawn they changed course again, now moving west toward the Yucatan Peninsula. Because of the almost constant rain visibility was reduced to less than a mile and, because of miserable weather, they saw no fishermen.

On the third day, the small convoy reached the Mexican coast near Bahía de la Ascención, a coastal region without any remarkable population. This was where they planned to board U-888....

49. Jibacoa, Cuba - July 29, 1945.

In the meantime, Ariana Herzog and Albert Krantz traveled from Berlin to Genoa, Italy, to find a ship which would take them back to Cuba. Using her Red Cross passports and some extra money, she had no problem getting a cabin on the top deck of an Italian freighter. During the trip across the Atlantic, they took their meals in their cabin and avoided contact with the few other passengers.

Arriving in Havana, they moved straight to Ariana's luxurious home in Jibacoa and called Heinrich Berger. He came to see them, accompanied by a dark-skinned Cuban with shiny black hair and a very thin moustache.

Krantz turned angrily to Berger, saying he didn't want to see any Cubans. Berger grinned. "Calm down, Don Alberto, this is one you always wanted to see. May I present Pluto to you? His real name is Armando Cuevas."

A devilish smile lit up Krantz's face as he shook hands with Pluto. "Just the man I need. It couldn't be better."

Berger explained that the OSS had actually sent Cuevas to Cuba to find Heinz and the SS men. They all laughed at the ignorance of the people in Washington who thought Pluto was such an asset to them. It was a good joke.

"Svensen has found U-888," Pluto said when the laughter subsided. "The bastard is towing it to Mexico. If we want to intercept, it will have to be soon."

"I need this U-boat to blackmail Truman and Attlee," said Krantz. We must rip it out of the American hands. It is imperative, you understand?"

"That's not going to be easy," Berger said.

Krantz laughed aloud. "It's nothing! The SS freed Mussolini from the Italians on the Mount Gran Sasso. So, we can free the U-888 from the Yankees."

Doggedly, they worked out the details of a plan to take over the salvaged U-boat. They would take an armed Cuban vessel, attack the sleeping Yankees and kill them all.

Armando suggested he would stay ashore to provide information about the Yankees.

Ariana spoke up. "Armando — Pluto — should not participate in the battle. He must be unseen by the Americans so he can return and continue his work in Washington."

Krantz flushed with anger. He had seen how Ariana and Armando exchanged looks, and he well knew about Ariana's appetites.

"No way!" he shouted. "*I* need him. That's it!"

"But think, Albert, how valuable to have a spy in the United States! You can't let such an opportunity be lost to us. Armando must remain behind."

Krantz banged his fist on the table. "Every one of us will fight on the sea! Understand?" Ariana didn't answer. She looked through the large window of her home over the white beach that smoothly curved around the blue bay. Disillusion showed on her face as she turned her head away from Krantz.

Krantz didn't see. He was too busy with his plans for victory, determined to win this time.

50. Bahía de la Ascención, Mexico - July 30, 1945.

It had been Abe Weinstein's decision that the sub be examined along the Mexican coast where there would be no interruptions from unwanted observers. So Erik sent the divers down to blow compressed air through openings in the diving tank bottom. Air bubbles rose into the diving tank and collected below the closed diving valve. The submarine rose slowly to the surface. First the conning tower and the ack-ack guns, then the deck of the submarine broke through the water. Finally they pumped the remaining water out of the conning tower room.

Four anchors, lowered by the ERNIE, were tied to U-888.

Now came the most frightening part of the assignment. The ten cylinders must be disconnected and loaded on the ALCONA, a U.S.Navy ship of 2,460 tons that would carry the containers to Johnston Island, eight hundred miles southwest of Hawaii. There they would be carefully examined by experts on germ warfare under the direction of Dr.Bernstein. The ALCONA was due August 10.

"Hans, if the containers are intact," Erik asked, "how long will it take to remove them from the deck?"

"Just a few hours."

"Okay, then we can do that shortly before the ALCONA arrives. Right now we'd better go inside the boat to retrieve documents."

Dr.Bernstein, who had donned a safety suit with a mask and breathing apparatus, was being rowed back to the sub in a dinghy. A sailor similarly attired pulled the oars.

They watched as Bernstein climbed the ladder to the conning tower and took air samples at the open hatch in small bottles. Then Bernstein disappeared in the conning tower room to open the hatch and take samples of the air inside the U-boat. After a few minutes he returned. Back on the ERNIE he opened his small field laboratory and began to work within the safe environment of its chamber, enclosing the ten small bottles and

179

all chemicals he needed for the analysis work.

After half an hour, he told the others, "Without any doubt a poison has developed inside the U-boat. In Germany we used to call it 'Churchill's Cigar Smoke.' A code name for stuff developed by a group of SS chemists working for Dr.Mengele. Sometimes the SS used it to kill political enemies after leaving them in a locked room. A devilish method of eliminating dissidents without firing a shot! It is a mixture of two harmless liquids fatal when combined. Amazing that it would be used on a U-boat against German sailors!"

"So that's how they did it!" Erik said. "They brought two harmless liquids on board and at the right time mixed them together. The guys on the sub didn't have a chance."

Bernstein nodded. "I suggest someone put on a safety suit and come with me. We'll remove the documents from the sub."

"I must show you where they are," Hans said. "Will the bodies of the crew be decomposed?"

"I doubt it. The poison will have killed all the bacteria in the enclosed room and even within the bodies. The bodies should be in good condition."

Erik made a quick decision. "I'll go with you. I want to see the crew and determine if there was a struggle in the boat before it sunk."

"It won't be a nice view," Bernstein warned.

The three men, breathing apparatus attached to their backs, stepped aboard the U-888. Brinker, the U-boat commander, the first to enter the boat, advised they climb down the ladder in the forward hatch above the galley. To his horror he almost trampled on the cook's small body which lay on the galley deck. Instinctively, Brinker said, "Excuse me..." until he became aware of the eerie situation. A few more steps took him to the petty officers' room. He directed the flashlight back and forth. With shock he discovered Schramm, the navigator, and the other petty officers sitting around the table. Schramm clutched his half-full beer bottle in his hand. Several others slumped on the table as if taking a nap; others leaned against the bunks. No sign of a struggle, nor of destruction. Brinker was tempted to talk to Schramm whose eyes stared right at him.

Wake up! The commander silently shouted to himself. These men are dead! He had to force himself to accept that. Hartmann sat at the navigator's side, his face turned as if still talking to him. Were their last words thoughts about their families?

Brinker understood that the families of his crew members would never see them again. Their children would never meet their fathers, the wives never embrace their husbands. Knowing all families, he felt sad about their sorrows. Grief about their fates and the loss of their loved ones overwhelmed the skipper. Tears rolled down his cheeks.

Erik and Bernstein stood besides Hans. Looking at each other through the glass plates of their helmets, the three men saw only horror on each other's faces.

Brinker uneasily walked to the officers' wardroom, where the same ghostly scene shocked him. The flashlight showed officers sitting around the table, beer bottles tipped over or still in their hands. Schroeder, the second watch officer, lay on the deck. The skipper touched the officer's arm. It was cold and stiff. In the spooky silence he heard his own breathing increased a hundred-fold in his helmet. Mmmmmmmmmmffffffffff-hahhhhhhhhhhh. Terror-stricken, he stared at *Oberleutnant* Topper, the chief engineer, who smiled as if telling a joke.

Brinker could no longer look at the officers. He felt sick. His feet refused to walk, his hands became stiff, cold sweat breaking out on his back. He forced himself to calm down and breathe slower. It's not hell, he told himself. It's a wax museum. Nothing to fear here. Sorrow? Of course. Guilt? No. Grief, yes. He had felt responsibility for these men.

He walked to the combat center. His steps sounded like sharp hammer blows on the metal deck, reverberating inside the submarine. Two sailors sat in front of the hydroplane handling wheels, their heads leaning against them. A machinist's body lay on the deck in front of the set of valves. Brinker remembered how this young man had once yelled, "*Auftauchen*! Surface! I want to get out! I hate the war. Do you hear? Surface!" — "Be quiet," the bosun had said. "It will be over in a few minutes." Now it *was* over. And he was dead. They all were dead.

Brinker shivered. Had he betrayed his men? He stood here as the only survivor. What had he done to survive? His hands began to tremble.

Brinker turned back to the wardroom. He moved the beam of his flashlight around. Where is the first watch officer? They had fought together on ten patrols. There he is. The officer's body was sprawled over the table, his hand holding half a cookie. He loved cookies, eating at least a dozen every day. So he died happy.

The skipper walked over to the radio shack. Here, there definitely had been destruction. The sub's radio was a mangled mess. Abert, the radio operator, sat in front of a small device, earphones on his head, hands at the knob of a primitive radio. The SS had destroyed the sub's voice. How stupid! If anyone could cobble up a new radio for them it would be Abert. In the corner was the small transmitter Abert used to send the messages the Dutchman had received and reported. Brinker reached down to the small metal safe in which he had stored the documents. He grabbed the yellow envelope and passed it to Russ.

Erik touched Brinker's arm and pointed his thumb up, signaling their return to the deck.

Back on the ERNIE and seated in the mess room with Erik, Brinker closed his eyes, trying to free himself from the horror he'd felt on his boat. Walking among his men, dead now for three months, had been a nightmare. He was convinced the crew had been killed by Krantz.

One of the sailors who doubled as radio operator entered the room with a decoded message from Washington and handed it to Erik.

> HOPE ETC. SPOTTED. NEW
> DESTINATION LITTLE CAYMAN ISLAND.
> RENDEZVOUS ALCONA 08/10/45. ABE.

This message brought Brinker back to reality. "I don't like

this," he said. "Towing the sub is dangerous. We can lose it."
They called Russ Bender and showed him the message. "Damn!
Must have seen us from shore," Erik said. "Do we tow the sub
as it is now?" he asked.

"Well, we certainly don't want to show the fact that we have
a German submarine in tow," Russ said.

"I can go aboard," Hans offered. "I'll open the diving valve
to let the air escape from the diving tank. Yet it is unsafe to tow
the sub in that condition."

"Secrecy is more important than safety," Russ said.

"I don't agree," Erik replied. "We can't lose the containers
now."

"Abe told us in Miami to keep this whole thing hush-hush."
Russ insisted. "He doesn't want the existence of a U-boat
carrying a lethal load of germs broadcast to the world."

"Towing a semi-submerged sub is hazardous. If its bow is
lowered, the downward trend can't be stopped. The reserve
buoyancy is too small."

"Imagine if we're seen towing a German U-boat through the
Pacific five months after the war! There's bound to be publicity.
Some newshound will get nosey. We can't risk that."

Erik sighed. "That's true. Okay then, let Hans lower the sub."

The skipper slid again into his safety outfit and went on board
the U-888. He closed the hatches at the bow and stern sections
and secured them by rotating the locking wheel, then stepped
through the turret hatch into the submarine.

From the HOPE Erik and Russ watched as air escaped from
the sub's diving tank and the submarine slowly submerged.
When the conning tower deck was about three feet above water,
Russ whistled three times — the signal for Brinker to close the
air valve. The sub kept the level and was ready to be towed.

51. Cienfuegos, Cuba - August 1, 1945.

Krantz, on board a ship which Cuevas had hired in the port of Cienfuegos, received daily information from Berger and Cuevas. He knew exactly where and when U-888 was discovered, towed away and boarded. Messages came in from several coastal agents in Cuba and Mexico. He heard of Brinker's participation with surprise.

"That bastard's alive!" he yelled. "Now I can finish him off!"

Krantz was really overwhelmed. How did he come out of that tin can? was his thought. Why is he the only one?

"That stupid commander must have a head of iron," he told Cuevas. "But he won't be a problem. Our bullets will take care of him soon enough."

"How long are you willing to wait?" Cuevas asked nervously. "What if they load the containers on the ALCONA before you act? I told you the Yankees plan to load them on that transport vessel. It will be a different story to challenge a naval ship. I don't like this delay. I say we act now. Do something!"

Krantz regarded him with contempt. "I'm in charge. *Halt Deine Fresse*! - Shut up! You have to wait until I give the order to attack, understand?"

"We must be careful. Our reports may be heard by the Yankees, as we overhear their messages. If you would only listen, you would be a better leader."

"Hey!" Krantz yelled. "I don't like the way you talk to me, understand? I'm not used to being told what to do. The Germans know how to obey orders. You lousy pigs still have to learn that."

Krantz was angry. Cuevas was too arrogant. As soon as U-888 was secured, he would have no further use for this spy. A stray bullet would remove Cuevas during the upcoming battle.

Only hours later, Krantz and Cuevas sailed toward the Mexican coast. The crew consisted of a Cuban captain, two machinists and eight SS officers from Berger's espionage group.

Krantz paced the deck, his excitement growing now that he was actually on his way to rescue the submarine and the miracle weapon. How fortunate the Americans had chosen a place so empty of people. Anchored offshore they would be sitting ducks. It made his job so much easier.

He laughed aloud at the thought that the Americans did all the work for him. Now he had only to kill the dummies, blow up their boats and take over the submarine. Then nothing would stand in his way. Briskly, he rubbed his hands and walked faster, his thoughts outracing his legs.

The world! He would conquer the world! He would carry on what Hitler started. The Miracle Weapon would help him rule the world!

52. Caribbean Sea - August 2, 1945.

The HOPE with the almost-submerged U-boat in tow sailed slowly through the Caribbean Sea toward the small Cayman Island one hundred fifty miles south of Cuba. Five hundred feet behind, the ERNIE followed. At dawn they were far from the coast and could no longer be seen by anyone on land. The rain had stopped and a haze hid them, allowing only a few miles of clear sight.

"We should be safe by now," Russ said to Erik, who organized a 'round-the-clock lookout. Every two hours the two on-duty crew members of the HOPE were relieved.

"Who do you think spotted us?" Erik asked.

"Mexicans? Curious about the sub?" Russ suggested.

"Possibly." Hans shrugged. "What if Krantz is on our tail?"

Russ whistled. "The SS from Cuba? Impossible."

"The way Hans told us, this Krantz is another Hitler," Erik said. "Maybe he wants the containers."

"Shit! And I thought this was going to be easy." Russ smiled.

Brinker supervised the towing. He insisted they travel no faster than three knots. "Any more speed and we run the risk of swamping her, even with the nets and the glass balls in place. The hatch is closed. But the sub's bow shouldn't be pushed down. We must have patience. Now that we have our prize, we don't want to lose it."

The next day brought more of the same. The slow speed had a depressing effect. The divers played cards with a sailor.

"Ship behind us!" a sailor shouted from the deck of the steering house.

Every one grabbed his binoculars and looked toward the west at the vessel approaching from the Mexican coast.

"It's three miles away," Hans said. "The damn haze was hiding it."

"Seems to be Mexican," Erik said. "Maybe Mexican Coast Guard. Shit!"

186

Slowly the ship came closer. They could make out a white ship with two masts and a yellow smokestack. The bridge had four windows. Since there was no smoke visible, it was probably run by diesel, Erik thought. No big bow wave showed.

"It's making about eight knots," the captain said.

"Maybe one hundred twenty feet long," Hans said. "It's larger and stronger than our wooden boats."

"They show the Mexican flag," the captain said, putting his binoculars down.

Erik saw Hans walk to the bow stowage room and return with two machine guns, which he stored below the steering console in the bridge room.

"Being prepared may save our lives," he said. He went back and forth, carrying ammo boxes and rifles, stowing them all around the boat.

"The typical soldier," Russ said. "Hans won't give up fighting."

Hans came back to the steering room. "I'm glad I covered the conning tower with a canvas," he said. "But why did I not cut off the periscope? Now it's too late."

The ERNIE kept its position between the U-boat and the Mexican vessel, which came closer.

"We can't take on the Mexican Coast Guard," Russ said. "We'll have to stop if they tell us to."

"Let's just play it by ear," Hans said.

Now the Mexican ship approached to four hundred yards behind the small convoy. It veered to starboard to pass alongside.

Erik, Russ, Hans and the captain on the HOPE still watched through their binoculars as the ship passed the ERNIE and the sub at a distance of about three hundred feet. No one could be seen on deck. Strange! Erik thought. When the ship was even with the HOPE, the door of the steering house opened. A man in a white navy uniform appeared. He shouted in Spanish through a megaphone, "Mexican Coast Guard. Stop! — Stop immediately!"

"Don't," Hans said to Erik and the captain. "The sub will run against us. The towing line will mess up our propeller."

The Mexican officer lifted his megaphone again and yelled, "*¿Qué toan?* What are you towing?"

"*Un barco dañado.* A damaged vessel," Erik shouted back.

"Drop the towing line! The vessel is Mexican property."

Erik gave no answer.

Russ thought about their legal situation. "We're more than three miles away from the Mexican coast," he said. "They haven't any right to commandeer us."

The coast guard vessel passed the HOPE and circled in front of it. Still, only one man was visible on deck. The ship had a long deck house with several windows and bull eyes. The elevated steering room and bridge allowed an all-around view for the captain. It was well-kept and looked freshly-painted. A green-white-red flag was hoisted at the rear mast's gaff.

"That doesn't look like a Mexican Coast Guard vessel," Erik said. "It's a private ship. It may be a luxury yacht of an American millionaire. See the name PABLO? Caution!"

Suddenly, a small rubber boat with outboard motor appeared, passing at high speed in front of the PABLO's bow. Probably they had lowered it at their starboard side, away from the HOPE, Erik decided. One man held the steering wheel, another sat in the front.

"Dammit! They want to board my U-boat," Hans said to Erik.

The rubber boat reduced speed and indeed went alongside the conning tower. The men jumped over, trampeled on the camouflage canvas and waved toward the PABLO, which still circled the small convoy.

"Hey! They'll be too damned close behind the ERNIE," Hans said.

Kroeeeeetchtchtch! With a loud screeching noise the PABLO crashed into the ERNIE's stern! The metallic bow of the white ship sliced open the wooden hull of the ERNIE. Then the ship pulled back. Two Mexican men stormed from its deck house and threw two cans on ERNIE's deck, followed by a Molotov cocktail. With a loud hiss, fire spread over the stern. A huge yellow-red-blue flame sprang up and a black cloud rose four hundred feet high. The PABLO pulled away faster from the burning boat. Then a terrible explosion rent the air and the ERNIE disappeared in a huge fireball. Debris flew in all directions. The pressure wave blasted the two men who stood on the bow of the PABLO back against the steering house where all windows were smashed. The ERNIE no longer existed.

"Oh God! They're gone," Russ exclaimed. "We're next! Let's fight! Hans was right!" He grabbed a machine gun and jumped on deck, kneeling behind the reeling. A sailor took an ammo box and knelt beside him.

Hans watched the men on the sub's turret. "They are opening the turret hatch," he yelled, pointing to the sub. They lifted their arm and yelled, "*Sieg Heil!*"

"Erik! The SS is here!" Hans called.

Shocked, Erik recognized what would happen. Had he erred? He saw the small man waving from the submarine to a tall guy on the stern of the PABLO who waved back. He heard the SS man yell: "We got it!" Then he disappeared into the submarine.

At that moment Erik knew: The SS got U-888! The next five minutes will decide between life and death!

Erik's heart hammered, his breath went as fast as an air compressor, and his hands perspired. He heard Hans shout, "There's Krantz!"

The skipper started shooting. Ten rounds flew to the Mexican ship and drummed against the hull. The tall guy ran for cover behind the deck house. Then ten more shots. More and more.

Erik looked back to port side through the rear window. He saw the PABLO slowing its reverse motion. Christ, will they now ram us? he thought. He looked at the submarine. The floating glass balls whirled against each other. He saw Hans shooting round after round. A hellish noise like a drummer's solo in a jazz band, a constant clatter. This commander is mad! he thought. He heard the glass behind him break, turned and saw the wood splinter. The SS are shooting at us! he realized. Erik grabbed the machine gun below the steering board. He checked to see if it was loaded, then aimed at the PABLO's deck house and pulled the trigger. The machine gun shook in his hands. Kill, kill, kill, he thought.

The PABLO increased its speed and rushed toward the HOPE, then ran its propeller in reverse to stop the vessel alongside the HOPE. Hans yelled to the captain: "Hard starboard! They're going to crash into us." The HOPE turned around.

Seconds later the PABLO's broadside banged against the HOPE's port side. Both ships tilted away from each other, then swung back. At that moment the attackers, shooting, jumped on deck of the HOPE.

For a second Erik saw Hans in the covered entrance of the bow storage room, invisible to the attackers, firing his machine gun. The older diver, on his knees beside the cover, fed him new ammo belts.

One of the men who jumped on deck was Krantz. A moment later, the man in the white uniform ran across the PABLO's deck.

"Cuevas! You here?!" Russ called.

"Please don't shoot!" Cuevas yelled. "I was hijacked by Krantz."

Turning, Krantz aimed his machine gun toward Cuevas and mowed him down. "You traitor! Go to hell!" he shouted. Bullets dyed Cuevas' uniform red before he collapsed.

Cuevas fighting on Krantz' side! Erik thought. He'd been a mole? I bet he betrayed us for years!

Hans, machine gun in hand, pointed his weapon at Krantz. Krantz, his face distorted by hatred, yelled, "You pig! Finally I got you!"

Bullets and red-yellow arcs ejected from the two guns. Both men were hit and fell down, unable to use their guns. They began to crawl toward each other. Erik jumped out of the steering house toward Krantz, stepped on blood and slipped, losing his balance. He slid to Krantz's side.

Krantz lifted his gun above him.

Is this my last moment? Erik thought. He quickly lifted his gun to protect his head. There was a strange metallic noise; both guns met in the air, then Erik's arms were pushed down. I want to live! he thought desperately. With the utmost effort he smashed his gun against Krantz's head again and again. Blood squirted over Erik's face and hand. The acrid smell of powder and diesel exhaust pierced his senses. Suddenly Hans appeared at his side and stabbed Krantz's body several times.

Hans, his pants ripped and dripping blood, limped over the deck. "It's over!" he shouted. He stared at the bloody face of the SS leader. "One of the worst criminals in the world is dead."

Erik looked around. "Where's the PABLO?" he asked. The ship had moved away from the HOPE. Probably no one had stopped the reverse motion on the ship. The PABLO's crew was dead. Then he saw it moving toward the submarine! Will it touch it? Erik thought. Seconds later, the unthinkable happened. With a dull thud the PABLO pushed against the hull of U-888. The sub tilted. Is the hatch open? Erik wondered. He saw water rushing in. The stream caught the man on the turret, who tried to hold on to the submerging bulwark. He was sucked into the boat. Hans shouted, "Now they're all gone!"

The turret was totally under water. Then the periscope disappeared.

"There she goes!" Erik shouted in despair. Air bubbles whirled up toward the water surface. The glass balls from the bow section went under, then suddenly popped up.

Hans disappeared into the storage room, returned and threw a handgrenade against the PABLO's hull. It ripped a hole in the side of the ship.

Everyone on board the HOPE watched. Speechless, motionless, HOPE's crew saw the PABLO listing and tilting. Slowly, its bow went deeper, its stern and propeller, still rotating with a loud whirr, stuck out of the water for a short while until it submerged. Ten seconds later, the PABLO inclined to starboard side and capsized awkwardly.

A strange silence settled over the HOPE. Erik now became

aware of a sharp pain in his left arm and leg. He had been hit by Krantz's bullets. Only now he understood that Hans Brinker, the U-boat commander, saved them by taking guns and ammo aboard the HOPE. Without them they all would be dead. The pain in Erik's left arm and thigh was becoming unbearable. Hans and the diver limped over the deck.

Suddenly a sharp, dull noise sounded below the sea. The HOPE jerked up a foot and then fell down again.

U-888 is caving in! Erik thought. Everything is lost!

Another dull sound from the deep water below them. Another and another.

"The containers are imploding!" Erik shouted. He counted ten muted explosions.

Two days later the HOPE was tied to the pier in Miami harbor. Abe Weinstein greeted the survivors and congratulated them.

"Hitler's terrible toy is gone," he said. "Experts told me that all germs were killed when the containers imploded at that water depth. The debris of the miracle weapon lies at six thousand feet and can no longer disturb mankind."

"The threat of a Neo-Nazi *Reich* under Albert Krantz is also over," Erik said.

"Listen!" Abe Weinstein said severely. "We have to keep everything secret. We can never talk about it. The world should never know about the danger it was in. The President ordered yesterday that all information about the miracle weapon is declared top secret and is to be sealed in the archives for fifty years."

Then he stepped over to Hans Brinker, U-888's commander, now on crutches, and shook his left hand. Brinker's right arm was hidden in white bandages. He became the only German sailor to receive the U.S. Purple Heart.

Abe approached Erik. "You did an outstanding job. No reward is good enough to thank you for your courage and perseverance. It was through your efforts that we had so much success. Now

I have a surprise for you." He turned around, waving to someone on the pier. Upon this signal a twelve-year-old, blond boy rushed over the gangplank.

Erik held his son Harald in his arms for a long time.

Other Books Available

from

AMADOR PUBLISHERS:

EVA'S WAR

A TRUE STORY OF SURVIVAL

EVA'S WAR:
A TRUE STORY OF SURVIVAL
by Eva Krutein

ISBN: 0-938513-09-5 [Trade $17]
ISBN: 0-938513-08-7 [Paper $9]
260 pp.

This gripping story of flight, refugees, privation, defeat, moral quandaries, growth and finally healing is strangely moving and compelling. It becomes a powerful anti-war statement from a woman's perspective. One year is recounted, beginning in January, 1945. Danzig, a Free City between the Great Wars, was seized by Hitler in 1939, and threatened by Soviet troops as Eva flees with her daughter.

They say that history is written by the winners, yet this bit of history comes from that nation which lost the war. Now that that nation is recovered and reunited, this sort of remembering is all the more important. And Eva Krutein is no loser. She and her family now live in California, where she is an accomplished musician and writer.

"A marvelously moving and often humorous real-life story... sad revelations, painful memories, excruciating experiences are tempered by compassion, love and a powerful, contagious optimism. Music permeates this tale."

-- Alfred-Maurice de Zayas, JD, PhD,
Senior Legal Officer, The United Nations, Geneva, Switzerland

"Her novel-like presentation makes for exciting reading. The story of German refugees has not been well covered, so this should find a p2lace in academic and public libraries."
-- THE LIBRARY JOURNAL

"Eva's account is one of fervent desire for peace in a setting of chaos, deprivation and horror... Yet EVA'S WAR is not exclusively about grief and guilt. It is about forgiveness, trust, accomplishment and love of life."
-- Thora Guinn, ALBUQUERQUE PEACE CENTER NEWS

"A gripping, unforgettable family odyssey through the terror of war and its aftermath. Definitely a page-turner... A different view of both the victors and the vanquished. One woman's spellbinding adventure in keeping her family intact."
-- Douglas Muir, author of TIDES OF WAR

"An excellent, provocative and important book."   --Laurel Speer

PARADISE FOUND, AND LOST
ODYSSEY IN CHILE
by Eva Krutein
ISBN: 0-938513-16-8 [Paper $11.00]
241 pp.

Sequel to EVA'S WAR, this book tells of the Krutein family's nine years in Chile, where they are warmed by the beauty of the land and the openness of the people. Eva is sensitive to social injustice and *machismo*, and senses the pending violence of revolution and counter-revolution.

As in EVA'S WAR, we see important world-events from a new perspective. These are real people, and the events described are not imaginary. The account mounts to its sharp climax -- the decision that the family must emigrate again.

"The family's personal events are intertwined with Chile's social and political history from 1950 to 1989. Krutein witnesses the suffering of children with no future and women under the thumb of machismo, which only fuels her commitment to fight such injustices."

-- PUBLISHERS WEEKLY

"The author's abundant love for people provides the source of her political understanding."

-- Cecilia Pollock
Citizens for Peace, Laguna Hills, CA

"A loving account of the two faces of Chile. A necessary reading, for those interested in social processes from the view of a 'foreigner,' who adopted the country as her own."

Juani Funez Gonzalez
School of Social Sciences
University of California, Irvine, CA

"This is a book in the great tradition of sensitive participant-observer foreigners, who by their perspective help reveal the essence of a culture."

-- Timothy F. Harding
Professor of Latin American History
California State University, Los Angeles
Coordinating Editor, LATIN AMERICAN PERSPECTIVES

FAR FROM THE ANGELS
A Tale of Revolutionary Mexico
by Ben Tarver
ISBN: 0-938513-11-7 [250 pp. $10]

A young *gringa* is rescued from Pancho Villa's raid on Columbus, New Mexico in 1916, and spirited into Chihuahua. She is forced to pass as a boy and live in squalor, then becomes a pianist/spy in a bordello, and in the end becomes a woman, and a *Villista*. This sweeping novel of passion, cruelty, triumph and tragedy, is rooted in historical fact and an uncommon awareness of our mere humanity.

Ben Tarver is a native of southern New Mexico. He is a noted playwright, screenwriter and professor at the University of Alberta, in Edmonton.

"Ben Tarver has crafted another beautifully detailed story of action, romance and drama, played against the gripping panorama of the Mexican Revolution. It will move you to tears and laughter."
-- Elaine Boies, editor & critic, STATEN ISLAND ADVANCE

"...a well-written and highly recommended story. It's in the same league as, for instance, the novels of B. Traven that were set in revolutionary Mexico."
-- J. G. Eccarius, THE STAKE, San Francisco, CA

"Tarver, a bred-in-the bone southwesterner, knows his milieu well, and brings the times, the Mexican revolution and his gutsy young heroine to roaring, bodacious life!"
-- Les Roberts, prizewinning author of SNAKE OIL
reviewer for THE CLEVELAND PLAIN-DEALER

"Tarver has more than done his homework on people, places and background forces swirling around the events he depicts in his novel, and in writing a rousing adventure story, he brings a whole era to life."
-- Laurel Speer, REMARK, Tucson, AZ

A WORLD FOR THE MEEK
A FANTASY NOVEL
by H. G. Z. Willson
ISBN: 0-938513-01-X [192 pp. $9]

A post-blast life-affirming fantasy, in which the lone survivor finds a baby in the kiva, rears him, loses him, goes Zen-crazy walking from Duke City to the Gulf of California, where he survives a very long time, and finds love and meaning among the dolphins and the octopi. When the dolphins find our Noah, they think they've found a fossil.

This fantasy novel is more in the tradition of *Gulliver's Travels* and *Robinson Crusoe* than the modern interplanetary invasion and star war craze. Here sensuality and curiosity have replaced violence and acquisitiveness. Willson is also the author of *This'll Kill Ya,* a modern anti-censorship fantasy romp.

"Magically written, and full of wisdom."   -- BOOKS OF THE SOUTHWEST

"...a magical flower of fantasy...eerie...transcendent. As we contemplate the very real prospect of a devastating near future, Willson's daring meditation through the destruction and out the other end is a wonderful affirmation. It is also an unusual and delightfully rendered story."   -- SMALL PRESS REVIEW

"...very readable...really entering a world where the ego is transcended."
     -- Northrup Frye, author & critic, UNIVERSITY OF TORONTO

"This wistful and eloquent book rivals Miller's CANTICLE FOR LEIBOWITZ. The devastated southwest landscape, and his subsequent idyll on the shores of the Pacific, are both compelling and vivid. This is speculative science fiction at its most tender and hopeful -- and fun to read, too."
     -- Gene H. Bell-Villada, author & critic, WILLIAMS COLLEGE

"Willson combines mythic material from several traditions: the Biblical Apocalypse, Native American wisdom, and flashes of Zen Buddhism."
     -- THE BLOOMSBURY REVIEW

"...original and fascinating, surprising and uplifting at once...an exercise in modern mythology, creating something grounded in our world and yet speaking to our problems on a more symbolic level...a good tale about the art of living."
     -- FACT SHEET FIVE

ANCESTRAL NOTES

A FAMILY
DREAM
JOURNAL

ANCESTRAL NOTES:
A FAMILY DREAM JOURNAL
by Zelda Leah Gatuskin

ISBN: 0-938513-17-6, 175 pp. [$10.00]

A collection of dream journal entries, poems, essays, short stories, and a drama — based on the author's investigations into, and her feelings about her family history and cultural identity. She explores the themes of Jewish spirituality, *shtetl* life in Europe, immigration to the USA, men's and women's traditional roles. Repeated references to spirits convey the sense that this inquiry is not only guided but demanded by ancestral souls. The book is illustrated with nine original collages by the author.

"With a deceptively simple yet strong voice, Gatuskin explores and celebrates what it means to be a Jew, to be a woman, and to be a member of the human race."
-- ANNE BARNEY, author

"This work is a collection of intensely personal stories, dreams, memories, histories, and collages by the author. They come at times perilously close to the world of psychosis, which always tells the truth about a secret. Such secrets are revealed only to a mind resonating with love for the sufferer. In the present instance firm sanity prevails throughout the revelations.

"As I began to read this work the shade of Franz Kafka fell across my shoulder, soon to be merged with the shades of Dostoyevsky, of Sholem Aleichem, and a myriad of my own memories dancing and grieving with those of the author. And that is strange, you see, for she and I are of different lineage, joined only in the mind by a common humanity.

"As I read on I wanted to bow before the author and kiss her feet. I wanted to weep with her and her ancestors. In the next moment I wanted to laugh with her in a triumph of the spirit over grief and pain. I put on her sister's clothes, but the door to the crematorium was shut to me, for I am not worthy. No other work I have ever read has had such an effect on me."
-- William J. Turner, M.D., Professor Emeritus of Psychiatry
State University of New York, Stony Brook, NY

"A chronicle of personal awakening...Here is a joyful, insightful, poignant, tough-minded celebration of the individual self as a swirling complexity of genetics, random chance and divine and earth-bound humor."